Freaky Fast
Frankie Joe

Freaky Fast Frankie Joe

LUTRICIA CLIFTON

Holiday House / New York

Copyright © 2012 by Lutricia Clifton
All Rights Reserved
HOLIDAY HOUSE is registered in the U.S. Patent and Trademark Office.
Printed and Bound in November 2012 at Maple Vail, York, PA, USA.

3   5   7   9   10   8   6   4   2

Library of Congress Cataloging-in-Publication Data

Clifton, Lutricia.
Freaky Fast Frankie Joe / by Lutricia Clifton. — 1st ed.
p. cm.
Summary: Twelve-year-old Frankie Joe Huckaby, forced to live with the father
he never knew, a stepmother, and four stepbrothers in Illinois, starts a delivery
service to finance his escape back to his mother in Texas, not realizing he is
making a better life for himself than he ever had with her.
ISBN 978-0-8234-2367-5 (hardcover)
[1. Stepfamilies—Fiction.   2. Family life—Illinois—Fiction.   3. Delivery
of goods—Fiction.   4. Mothers and sons—Fiction.   5. Community
life—Illinois—Fiction.   6. Illinois—Fiction.]   I. Title.
PZ7.C622412Fr 2012
[Fic]—dc23
2011019976

ISBN 978-0-8234-2867-0 (paperback)

for Jeffrey and Christopher

Acknowledgements

Special thanks to my agent, William Reiss, for his encouragement and support. Special thanks also to my editor, Julie Amper, at Holiday House for her guidance and patience.

Saturday, September 19
The Lone Star Trailer Park, Laredo, Texas

10:00 A.M.

I don't like the way some of our neighbors look at me when I walk past. Mom calls them meddling busybodies because they sit on their front porches and whisper all the time—just like they're doing now. "Oooh, there's that boy," they're probably saying. "You know, the one whose mother was in the newspaper."

I sit down at the picnic table outside Mrs. Jones's trailer. Mr. O'Hare and Mr. Lopez are already there. They know about Mom, too, but they're my friends so they don't say anything. They want my last day to be fun.

"Look what I made, Frankie Joe." Mrs. Jones brings out a cake. Chocolate with rainbow frosting that spells out HURRY BACK HOME.

I think Mr. Lopez must have had a hand in decorating it. He's a house painter—only he calls himself a "house artist." He's a nut for wild colors. If he can't find a color he likes, he mixes his own. Sometimes he lets me

1

help do the mixing. He says I have a good eye for color. He lets me help name them, too.

"And something to wash it down." Mr. O'Hare hands me a glass of punch. He smiles at me, and his face folds up in wrinkles. His skin is brown as leather because he spends every day in the Chihuahua Desert. When he was a mechanic in the air force, Mr. O'Hare traveled all over the world. That's why he doesn't have a family of his own—because he was always moving around. He told me once that I was the grandson he never had. I've learned all about the places he's been to.

I take a big gulp of punch. Guava and strawberry, I think.

"Have another piece," Mrs. Jones insists. "You have a long trip ahead of you." Strings of white hair stick to her forehead. Though it's September, it's ninety degrees in the shade. While I eat, they talk.

"We'll watch out for your trailer," Mr. Lopez says. He's not wearing his painter's cap, so his forehead is half-white and half-brown.

Mr. O'Hare nods. "Like a hawk."

"Maybe I'll paint the front steps while you're gone," Mr. Lopez says. "They're in bad shape—could get a splinter if you're not careful."

Mom worked split shifts at the café. Mornings some days, evenings others. She didn't make a lot of money, so there wasn't a lot left over to fix up our place. She didn't worry about it because she said we weren't going to be here much longer. "This dump is just a stepping stone to something better," she said.

"I'll take care of the splinters," Mr. O'Hare says, looking at Mr. Lopez. "I have just the tool for that. You take care of the painting."

"That'd be great," I say, glad to have such good friends.

"I know how you feel about writing, but let us hear from you now and then." Mrs. Jones puts another piece of cake on my plate. "Maybe a Christmas card?"

I nod. Between chocolate cake and rainbow frosting and punch, I'm on a sugar high. I eat like it's my last meal.

Mr. Lopez looks at his watch. "Better open your presents now, Frankie Joe. Your dad's gonna be here soon."

"Presents...but..." I never expected a party *and* presents.

"Well, not real presents," Mrs. Jones says. "They're more like mementos."

A retired librarian, Mrs. Jones is a real stickler for words. I started staying with her after school when I was younger, and she read to me a lot—adventure books were my favorite. She won't allow a TV in her trailer because she thinks it's a bad influence. Her bookshelves are running over because the new librarian gives her "retired" books. Her son and his family live in England, so she doesn't get to see them much. She would invite me over to stay on nights when Mom worked late or went out with her friends.

She hands me a rectangle-shaped package wrapped in red tissue paper. The paper's probably recycled from Christmas, but it fits right in with the rainbow cake and guava-strawberry punch. I know it's a book before I open it.

"*Kidnapped!*" My favorite book! It's about this guy who leaves home and gets kidnapped by thugs and has to escape. A lot of the words were hard for me, but Mrs. Jones helped me when I got stuck.

"It's great," I tell her.

"Just a reminder of all our good times," she says. Her eyes begin to look wet, but I don't say anything. I don't want to make her sadder.

"Open mine next." Mr. O'Hare hands me a brown paper bag. Another book, I can tell from the shape. But it's floppy, not stiff like the other one, so I know it's not a retired library book.

"*Woo-hoo.*" It's one of Mr. O'Hare's field guides to rock collecting. "This is great, too!"

"When you get back, we'll find it," he tells me. "We won't stop looking till we do."

"It" is a space rock, a meteor that broke up when it fell out of the sky over the Chihuahua Desert. Mr. O'Hare looks for pieces of it every day, and I go with him when I can.

"Maybe you'll find some new kinds of rocks up there

4

in Illinois," he says. "You bring them back, we'll add them to our collection." Rocks are lined up clear around his trailer—sandstone, granite, limestone—all kinds of rocks.

"Yeah, I'll look for some new ones."

Mr. Lopez looks at his watch again and hands me a stiff piece of paper. "I didn't wrap mine 'cause it's color-ful enough."

I grin because he's right. It's a strip of paint samples showing some of his "creations."

"Maybe you'll see some new colors on your trip," he says. "You tell me about them when you get back—to inspire me."

"Thanks, Mr. Lopez. I'll keep an eye out."

He taps his watch, and I know it's time to leave.

"Well, I guess I gotta go." I thank them again for the party, my throat so tight I can hardly speak. "See you ... soon."

"I know it seems like a long time, Frankie Joe," Mr. O'Hare says. "But the time will fly by."

Mr. Lopez nods. "Yeah. July will be here before you know it."

"Look upon it as an adventure." Mrs. Jones's eyes are running over now. "Just pretend you're looking for treasure." Her eyes go round. "Oh dear, maybe I should have given you *Treasure Island*."

Everyone laughs.

"Yeah, adventure," I say, laughing like I'm excited, too.

But as I take my mementos back to our trailer to pack in my suitcase, I don't feel excited. I feel sad and a little scared. I don't want to leave my friends and go live with my dad. What if he doesn't like me? What if I don't like him?

11:15 A.M.

"Hello there, Frankie Joe," the man says, getting out of a Chevy van with Illinois license plates. "I'm your dad." He's tall and has red hair, the same color as mine, and freckles on his nose like I do.

"I figured," I say. I'd never known I looked like my dad. I couldn't remember anything about him.

Well, not much. There were birthday and Christmas cards when I was little. Mom would read them to me and show me the money that was tucked inside, then we'd go out on the town. New jeans and shirts for me. A cheeseburger at McDonald's for both of us. And sometimes, a Blizzard at the Dairy Queen.

He looks at the country back of our trailer, which borders on the Chihuahua Desert. "Well, your mother always wanted to go to faraway places." He shakes his head slightly. "Looks like she succeeded."

I don't say anything.

He looks at me. "I can't believe those people at the courthouse left you on your own."

"I stay by myself all the time. It's no big deal."

His face wrinkles up in a frown. "Well, it's a big deal

to me. There are rules about leaving a child on his own like that."

Rules. My head starts to throb like I'm coming down with the flu.

When I don't respond, he shakes his head. "Did you say good-bye to your friends?" He looks around the trailer park. "I didn't see many kids when I drove in. Looked like mostly retired people."

I look around, too. "Yeah, I guess...but I've got friends. They ride a different bus home so I see them at school mostly."

He sighs. "Okay then, let's get your stuff." He looks surprised when I load my suitcase and bike into the back of his van. "This all you've got?"

"Yes sir."

"What about the money I sent for your birthday? You know, for a new bicycle. That thing's sure not new."

"You sent money for my birthday...*this* year?" He doesn't answer. Instead, his mouth goes straight as a plank, and he jerks his thumb in the direction of the passenger-side door.

"I need to be back on the job by Monday," he says as he climbs into the van, "so we'll just be making pit-stops. You know, to fill up with gas and hit a McDonald's for takeout."

"I like McDonald's."

"Plan on using the toilet there, too. We've got a lot of ground to cover." He starts the engine. "I'll probably pull over at a Walmart™ down the road, catch some shut-eye."

"Um, maybe we can get a Blizzard at the DQ, too. You know, for dessert?"

Like Mom and I did when I used to get birthday cards from him.

"A Blizzard? Yeah, guess we can do that." He turns the air conditioner to high. "A lot hotter down here than I thought it would be. Something cold would be good."

Great. Maybe this will be an adventure after all.

"You had lunch?" he asks.

"Yes sir."

Cake and punch—a *lot* of cake and punch.

"Good, that'll save us some time. Buckle up."

We leave the Lone Star Trailer Park and wind our way through Laredo's streets, littered with trash and lined with low adobe buildings the color of dirt. The van's wheels churn up clouds of dust that have blown in from Mexico, which is only a stone's throw to the south.

Before long we've left Laredo in its brown-paper-bag colored dust. It becomes clear pretty quick that my dad isn't much of a talker. I'm not, either, so it's okay with me. I'd rather look out the window. Maybe I'll see some of the places that Mr. O'Hare has talked about.

2:45 P.M.

A few miles down the road, I see a sign that says AUSTIN— it's the capital of Texas. I'm excited because I want to tell Mr. O'Hare that I saw the capitol building...but we keep driving, bypassing the city.

Sagebrush green...cactus green. As the country goes by, I remember my promise to Mr. Lopez to look for new colors. I decide he would know these already. Besides, he likes bright colors, and these are anything but.

The van begins to feel quiet—too quiet. "Wanna listen to the radio?"

"Tried that coming down. Poor reception." He glances at my suitcase in the back of the van. "Didn't you bring any books to read...maybe some puzzles?"

I shake my head no. I have the book Mrs. Jones gave me, but it's a memento. So is Mr. O'Hare's. Besides, I don't like to read and I never do puzzles.

"You can be navigator then." He nods at a stack of road maps on the console.

"You used all these maps?"

"I get them free from Triple A."

The map for Texas is lying open. He's marked the route with a yellow highlighter, so there isn't any real navigating to do. I look at the other maps. Oklahoma. Missouri. Illinois. More yellow highlighter. I go back to looking at the country rolling by.

6:30 P.M.

We pick up cheeseburgers and drinks at a McDonald's near the Dallas/Fort Worth junction—a chocolate shake for me and a large iced tea for my dad. I can see tall buildings sticking up to the east, but we keep driving north.

"Crops look pretty good here," he says, between chewing.

"Huh?"

"The alfalfa and sugar beets, winter wheat." He points to crops in the fields we're passing. "They look pretty good."

"I guess," I say, looking out the window.

Alfalfa green...sugar-beet green...winter-wheat green. I wonder if Mr. Lopez would like any of these colors.

Nah, too dull.

We stay on I-35 all the way through Texas. I'm bored—nothing but green. I'm not much of a talker, but I almost ache to have a conversation with someone—anyone.

"So what am I gonna do while you're at work?" I'm thinking about the rock-hound book that Mr. O'Hare gave me, wondering if meteors fell out of the sky over Illinois.

"You'll go to school, of course. I called your school counselor yesterday morning, asked her to send your records on. I expect they'll be waiting when we get there."

"I gotta go to school in Illinois." It's more a statement than a question.

"Well, sure." He gives me a look. "Why wouldn't you?"

Well…" I suck the spit from the gap between my front teeth. "I was hoping I could just skip this year since I won't be staying permanently. You know, pick up when I get back home."

I hate school, and Mom doesn't seem to set much store by it, either.

"Doesn't matter how long you'll be staying," he says, eyeing me again. "Those are the rules."

"Um," I mumble, my mind racing. "I thought Mom was the only one who could get my records."

"Took care of the legalities yesterday morning, too. Signed papers making me your temporary legal guardian."

I'm out of arguments.

"School started a couple of weeks ago. Shouldn't take you long to catch up, if that's what you're worried about."

I go back to looking at country that's fenced off in green rectangles and squares. I'd rather explore the brush country back of the trailer park, which goes on for miles and miles. It's space too big to be fenced in.

10:00 P.M.

"Iced tea—heavy on the ice," he says into the speaker. "And a chocolate milk shake and an order of fries."

We've stopped at a lot of McDonald's since we left

Laredo, and he always orders the same thing because he's "parched." Iced tea, heavy on the ice.

"I'll be pulling off at a Walmart outside Oklahoma City," he says while we wait for our order. "It's a safe place to catch a few hours' sleep." He nods toward the McDonald's. "Better hit the restroom; last stop tonight."

"Yes sir." When I get back to the van, I hear him talking on his cell phone. He's telling someone when to expect him home.

Home? I become curious.

"Who's that you called?"

"My family...my wife and sons—my *other* sons. Haven't been able to reach them until now."

"You have other sons?"

"Four. Didn't your mom tell you?"

Four! I'm speechless.

"Buckle up," he says.

10:30 P.M.

Ten miles farther on, we pull off at a Walmart and park beneath one of their big halogen lights. There's nothing but a pool of black beyond the light, so I can't even see the skyline of Oklahoma City.

"You take the backseat," he says. "I'll take the front."

I stretch out on the backseat, but I can't stop the questions from squirming around in my head. Finally they worm their way out.

"What am I supposed to call her? Your new wife, I mean."

He takes his time answering. "Her name is Lizzie. But she probably won't mind if you call her Mom. That's what the boys call her."

"I'll call her Lizzie." Mom is what I call *my* mother. "What are the boys' names—my stepbrothers?"

"Well, actually they are your half brothers. Matthew's the oldest—next to you, that is. We call him Matt for short. Then there's Mark, Luke, and John—mostly he's called Little Johnny."

"You mean, like in the Bible?"

"It's a tradition in Lizzie's family. They're into names that withstand the test of time, not goofy names. No one's gonna forget what the Huckaby boys' names are, that's for sure."

Goofy names. I wonder if he thinks Frankie Joe is goofy. Why he didn't give me a name that would withstand the test of time? All at once, I realize I don't even know *his* name.

"So, what's your name? I mean, all Mom ever called you was FJ—when she spoke of you at all, that is."

"It's Franklin. Franklin Joseph Huckaby, same as yours." He's quiet for a couple of minutes. "It was your mom's idea to name you that, and..." He pauses. "Even as a baby, you had my hair, my eyes, so..." He glances away, then back at me. "So you've got my name. If you want, you can call me Dad."

"I see," I say, but I don't really. I'm wondering why my name wasn't his idea. "Thanks, but I'll call you FJ."

He remains quiet for several more minutes. "I tried to keep in touch, but...well, I got busy with things."

I translate "things" to mean his new wife and four other sons.

"And there's something else..." His voice sounds funny, like he's choking on a french fry. "Lizzie's the only wife I ever had. *Legal* wife, that is."

"Uh-huh," I say. "What exactly does that mean?"

"It, uh, it means your mom and I never got married."

I understand. His other sons are legitimate, and I'm not.

"But we used my name on your birth certificate," he says. "So legally, your name is Huckaby." He looks at me. "Okay?"

I say okay, but I don't feel better. I stare out the window at dark space lit up by an eerie white light, feeling like I've been kidnapped. Then I remember that it won't be for long—only ten months. Just until Mom gets out of jail.

Sunday, September 20

"Are we there yet?" I rub the sleep from my eyes.

"Not by a long shot."

A sign alongside the road tells me we are now on I-44. A different Triple-A map is lying open on the console, and I discover we're in Missouri, west of St. Louis.

FJ pulls into a drive-through at the next McDonald's. "Hop out and wash up. I'll get breakfast sandwiches to go."

When I get back, he folds up the Missouri map and hands me another one. "We'll be crossing into Illinois soon."

Back on the road, I see corn growing—really tall corn—and something else I don't recognize. "What's that stuff?" I point to bushy plants growing in arrow-straight rows that alternate with the cornfields.

"That? Why, that's soybeans. Corn and soybeans are the major crops here. They pay the bills."

I stare at him.

"I work as a grain inspector for the state," he explains. "Farmers have to comply with laws to make sure what they grow is safe for consumption and other uses. I visit farms, inspect grain for quality, and analyze it for chemical content. Round here, that *grain* is corn and soybeans."

"So...you're pretty important, huh?"

"Well, it's an important job. Making sure grain doesn't contain bacteria and disease is a big responsibility." He nods out the window. "Corn and soybeans are what puts the food on our table."

I look out the window again, imagining corn and soybeans on the table. Sometimes I make bean burritos for Mom's supper. Refried beans rolled up in a corn tortilla that I warm up in a skillet.

"You like burritos?"

"Burritos?" He pauses. "Not really, least not as a regular diet. Why?"

"Oh, nothing." I'm disappointed because I want him to like burritos, too. Then I decide that it's okay if he doesn't, because Mom does. I decide to fix her bean burritos the minute she gets back home.

2:45 P.M.

We exit I-39 North and weave our way down narrow asphalt roads that run alongside big white farmhouses and huge red barns and tall metal silos painted blue.

Silo blue…barn red. Finally! Colors Mr. Lopez will like. I can hardly wait to describe them to him.

A few minutes later, we pass a sign pointing the way to Chicago. "Aren't we going through Chicago?"

Mr. O'Hare has told me about Chicago. It's called the Windy City, and the street vendors sell Chicago dogs—hot dogs with tomatoes and dill pickles on them.

"Bypassed it." He points toward the east. "Chicago's that way, on Lake Michigan."

Great. I missed Chicago, too.

Out the window, I see herds of cows penned up next to red barns. Not skin-and-bone cows like those in Texas—huge black-and-white cows. Some with spots all over like dalmatian dogs; some with white stripes around their middles like Oreo cookies.

"That's dairy cattle," FJ says as I crane my neck looking at them. "Some farmers still keep a few on their farms. Most dairies are run different these days, though. Cows are kept in big barns, never let outside. Lights are kept burning all night to improve milk production. Did you know that? That light improves milk production? At night the barns look like flying saucers that have landed in the middle of the cornfields."

Cool. Things are looking up.

"How far is it to those barns? Close enough to bike?"

He gives me a look. "That would be trespassing. Besides, can't go disturbing the cows—could affect milk production."

17

My adventure is feeling like a roller-coaster ride.

"Well, here we are," he says, tapping a spot on the map. He slows down as we pass a sign that says CLEAR-VIEW. "We are now five miles from the Wisconsin state line. Wisconsin's known as the Dairy State. They make a lot of butter and cheese up there."

Clearview is circled on the Illinois map, and I can see that it's right at the top of the state. We've almost driven across the entire country, from bottom to top.

Just past the town sign is another one that says BUSI-NESSES IN CLEARVIEW. I glance at the dozen-or-so names on the sign. There isn't a McDonald's or DQ or Taco Bell or movie theater listed. Not even a Walmart. In fact, I don't recognize the name of a single one of the businesses on the sign.

"Where's the McDonald's?" I ask, feeling panicky.

He laughs. "Don't have one."

"Dairy Queen?"

Another laugh. "Have to drive twenty-five miles east or west to find a McDonald's or a DQ."

Twenty-five miles? Why would anyone want to live in such a place?

He reads my mind. "Clearview is close to my work. And it's a good place to raise kids. First-class school district, good things for kids to do. You know, like Scouts and 4-H."

"Uh-huh," I mumble.

"That's the school you'll go to." He points to a sprawling yellow-brick building. "There's three wings for the different grades. Primary, Middle School—that's fifth through eighth—and High School. The primary and middle-school principal's name is Mr. Arnt. We'll get you registered tomorrow."

I look at the side streets that run off the main one, hoping to see something that looks familiar. The two-story homes on the side streets have porches that stretch around the front and sides of the house. There isn't a dirt clod or scrap of trash anywhere.

FJ turns off the main street and drives a couple of blocks. Not as much as a candy-bar wrapper clutters the gutter in front of the two-story house with green shutters where he parks the van. On the front porch, I see shiny, new-looking bikes lined up and remember the money he supposedly sent for my birthday.

I don't care, I think. I bet my bike's every bit as good as those—no, *better*.

In a field at the end of the block, I see corn and soybeans growing.

"Where do your kids ride their bikes?"

"Why, on the street. But there is a park a few blocks away with a paved bike path, in case you'd rather ride there."

Paved bike path? The Chihuahua Desert doesn't have an unpaved bike path, much less a paved one.

"Meteors ever fall out of the sky around here?"

"Meteors?" He looks confused.

I was afraid of that.

3:30 P.M.

Four boys burst out the front door and grab FJ around his shoulders, arms, middle, and knees.

Matt, Mark, Luke, and Little Johnny.

They're wearing T-shirts and jeans like I am, except theirs are clean. Mine have mustard and catsup and grease down the front and are wrinkled because I've worn them for two days.

The second-shortest boy wears glasses, but other than that, the four legitimate Huckaby sons look pretty much the same. I don't look anything like them. Their eyes are chocolate brown, not blue like mine; their hair and eyebrows are thick and brown, too.

I hear a door slam again. A short, round woman with curly brown hair and chocolate-brown eyes runs down the front steps. She's dressed in slacks and a plaid shirt, which billows when she stretches out her arms. A tent with legs.

Lizzie.

Mom is about as opposite of her as you can get. Mom's hair is short and blond, all shiny and spiky, and she likes capri pants and bright T-shirts. Lime green is her favorite color because her eyes are green. Sometimes she paints her fingernails and toenails to match what she's wearing. Just thinking about her makes me homesick.

Squealing like car brakes when someone stomps on them, Lizzie reaches over the four boys and grabs FJ around the neck. I wonder how he's able to breathe, but he just gathers them up in his long arms as if trying to squeeze the life out of them. When he lets them go, they turn and stare at me.

"Hey." I nod, holding tight to my suitcase.

"Oh, yeah," FJ says. He walks over to me, puts his arm around my shoulders. "This is Frankie Joe, my... my oldest son."

"That's why he's named after you," the boy with glasses says. "Right, Dad? 'Cause he's the oldest."

"Does that mean he can boss us around?" the smallest boy asks. "Like Matt does?"

"Do not," the tallest boy says.

"Do too! 'Cept now, he can boss *you* around."

"Can *not*."

"Can too—"

"Enough of that." Lizzie gives me an ear-to-ear grin. "Why, he's the spitting image of you, FJ." She frowns suddenly. "Except he's thin—way too thin."

My face burns. What does she mean, too thin? Mom always told me I was tall for my age and would fill out sideways when I stopped growing skyways. I begin to squirm, waiting for someone to notice that I'm just tall for my age. But FJ and Lizzie say nothing, while the four boys just stare at me some more.

Finally Lizzie cuts short the staring, saying, "I can fix thin. People don't stay thin for long in *my* house."

Before I can blink, she's pulling me up the steps, the half brothers hot on my heels like a posse keeping herd on me.

I brace myself for my first meal of corn and soybeans.

3:55 P.M.

Lizzie sets out a spread the likes of which I've never seen before: crispy fried chicken, mashed potatoes with cheese sprinkled on top, gravy shiny with pan drippings, orange Jell-O with shredded carrots, hot rolls with butter, and apple pie for dessert.

"Did Frank tell you I'm a quilter, Frankie Joe?" Lizzie smiles at me.

I figure out that FJ is Frank and shake my head no.

"My Quilt Circle meets here every Saturday afternoon. A quilt takes hours and hours to make. My quilts have won many a blue ribbon at the county fair."

"The fair is held every August," FJ explains. He helps himself to another helping of chicken and lets Lizzie talk on.

"I work part-time at the JCPenney store, that's in the next town over. But I'm home by six o'clock, soon after the boys get home from The Great Escape—that's what the after-school program is called." She pauses to catch her breath. "I get a fifteen-percent discount on anything I buy, which helps out a lot with four boys growing like weeds."

Lizzie smiles around the table at her four "weeds," who respond with ear-to-ear grins of their own. I notice she stops short of giving me a grin, and I wonder what I am if not a "weed."

"I'm the best colorer in first grade," the youngest boy says, taking over. He's the one called Little Johnny. "My teacher puts all my pictures up in the room for everyone to see 'cause I never color outside the lines."

"I'm really good at math," Luke says next. He's the one who wears glasses. He announces that he plans on being a "gazzillionaire" when he grows up. "I can count to a hundred, and count by twos, and count by threes, and count by fours, and count by fives. I can even count by sevens!" He looks at me. "Can you count by sevens?"

I stare at him, wondering what's so important about counting by sevens.

"Of course, he can count by sevens," Lizzie says, laughing. "Frankie Joe's twelve years old."

"I'm the smartest one of all," Mark chimes in. "I skipped third grade and went straight to fourth. I have an excellent brain. You like games? We have a Game Boy. What's your favorite game? Bet I can beat'cha."

That would be a safe bet. A couple of my friends back in Laredo have Game Boys, but Mom doesn't make enough money to buy me one. Besides, who needs pretend games? I'd rather do real things—like help Mr. Lopez. Or important things—like finding space rocks with Mr. O'Hare.

"I don't play those games," I tell him.

"You don't play games!" Mark looks at me like I've just admitted to crossing the Rio Grande illegally. "We knew you'd be a freak!"

Freak? So that's why I'm not a "weed." I'm a freak.

"More potatoes, Frankie Joe?" Lizzie shoots Mark a look to kill as she plops more potatoes on my plate. I concentrate on eating, listening to the rest of them talk. Which, except for FJ, they sure like to do.

Oldest-brother Matt is the least talkative of all the brothers. I learn that he's in the fifth grade, but he makes no announcement about being the best at anything. What bothers me about him is the way his eyes spark when he looks at me. They're like two chunks of smoldering charcoal, ready to ignite. I haven't been here thirty minutes, and already I feel like I've stepped on his toes.

"So," Lizzie says, "tell us what you're good at Frankie Joe?" She gives me the big smile again.

Everyone grows quiet, waiting for me to speak. I feel myself blink. And blink some more. I blink a lot before FJ takes over.

"That's enough talk for now. It's been a long trip, and Frankie Joe's got to be worn down to a nub. I know I am." He looks at me. "You get enough to eat?"

24

"Yes sir." I've had seconds on everything—even thirds on fried chicken. If corn and soybeans were any part of the meal, I don't know which part it was.

I turn to Lizzie. "It was good."

Her eyes glow. "If you want a snack later, I made cookies. Chocolate chip."

Chocolate chip!

Mom bought packaged cookies, Oreos mostly because that's her favorite kind. She doesn't eat sweets much, though. She's been on a diet as long as I can remember. "Guys don't like fat girls," she told me once when she was getting ready to go out on a date.

"Chocolate chip's my favorite," I tell Lizzie.

Even if I am the freak in the bunch, I begin to think Clearview, Illinois, might not be a bad place to bunk... for a few months.

5:05 P.M.

"Matt and Mark share a bedroom, you see." FJ talks as we make our way upstairs, the posse of half brothers right behind us. He opens a door to a room on the second floor.

I see two corner desks loaded down with schoolbooks. Math. History. Science. English. Under bunk beds, I see a Battleship game and a Game Boy, plus a stack of disks.

Four alien-looking creatures wearing eye masks leer at me from the wall: a *Teenage Mutant Ninja Turtles* poster. Mom took me to see the movie when it came out. The four dark-eyed half brothers remind me of the turtles.

I eye the crowded room, wondering if I'll be sleeping on the floor. On the drive from Laredo, I never dreamed I would be sharing a bedroom with one mutant ninja, much less two—and sleeping on the floor.

"Luke and Johnny share another room," FJ says. He opens the door across the hall. "The rooms are small, you see."

Inside are two more desks, crayon drawings taped on the wall, books and games stuffed under bunk beds—and another *Teenage Mutant Ninja Turtles* poster. It makes sense: FJ tests grain for chemicals, and the ninja turtles mutated because of toxic waste. I figure I'll be hearing *kowabunga, dude!* a lot.

"Uh-huh," I mumble, looking at the floor again for space to roll out a sleeping bag. When FJ walks farther down the hall to another door, my heart starts doing flip-flops.

Cool. I get my own bedroom.

But through the door, I see a flight of steep, narrow, dark stairs and have another thought: *Dope, they're gonna to stick you in a dark, drafty attic.*

"So," FJ says as we climb. "We thought—Lizzie and me, that is—that this might be better for you. Being the other rooms are so small."

"Uh-huh," I mumble. I know small rooms are not

the reason I'm being isolated. It doesn't take an excellent brain to figure that out.

"You can use the boys' bathroom there on the second floor. Lizzie and I use the one on the first...and it doubles as the guest bathroom."

The steps are steep. I bounce my suitcase off the wall like a basketball. Reaching the top, I step into a large, open space. Walls slant to a peak and there are windows on opposite ends. An old metal bed sits under the back window, and beside it is a chest with an alarm clock on it. A small desk sits under the other window, a bookshelf beside it, and a calendar on the wall. Cardboard boxes stacked in between tell me that the attic is normally used for storage.

All this is mine? It's bigger than our trailer in Laredo!

FJ says, "You think this'll do all right? I mean, you're just here temporarily, you know."

I like the sound of that word *temporarily*.

"Yes sir," I say. "This'll do all right."

"Stairs are hard on Lizzie," FJ says. "You'll need to run the vacuum and keep things picked up. Change the sheets once a week and carry them downstairs to the laundry room. But take your dirty clothes down every day so Lizzie can keep up with the wash. She'll iron your clothes and fold your socks and underwear. You'll need to haul them back upstairs. The other boys have to do the same thing."

Ironed clothes? Folded underwear? At home I use things right out of the dryer.

"That clear, Frankie Joe?"

"Yes sir."

"Those all the belongings you got?" Matt points to my suitcase. The ninja posse is clumped by the stairs, watching us.

"Well, except for his bicycle," FJ says. "Guess we might as well unload that, too."

5:40 P.M.

I watch as FJ hauls my bicycle out of the van.

Matt looks at me. "That's your bike?"

"But...but that can't be," Lizzie sputters. "We sent money to—"

FJ shoots Lizzie a fast look, and the rest of her words fade away. "Here you go, Frankie Joe," he says. "Set your bike up there on the porch with the others."

As I wheel the old ten-speed up the sidewalk, I feel like a germ under a microscope. The bike had been bright yellow when it was new, and up close, traces of yellow can still be seen among the dents and scrapes and rust. The words *Rover Sport* are partly legible on the frame.

"Isn't that a girl's bike?" Little Johnny asks. "The girls at school have bikes with baskets on the front, just like that."

The ninja posse laughs.

"No, it's not like that," I say, feeling my face turn hot. "I just put this basket on the front so I could haul stuff. But it's not a girl's bike."

Mark asks, "Where'd you get that thing?"

My face gets hotter. "I found it in a trash Dumpster. Rich snowbirds that go south in the winter throw things away they don't want to haul back. I figure some guy wrecked it out in the desert. Mr. O'Hare helped me fix it up, but I earned the money for new tires myself."

"You're a Dumpster diver?" Mark looks at his brothers and laughs. "He's a Dumpster diver!"

"That's enough, Mark," FJ says.

"How'd you earn the money for new tires?" Luke asks.

I remember that he's the one who wants to be a "gazzillionaire." He examines the fat tires on my bike, twice as big as the skinny racing tires on theirs.

"I run errands and haul things for people. You know, pick up groceries for Mrs. Jones or smokes for Mr. Lopez. They're my neighbors at the Lone Star Trailer Park where we live. They give me tips, which Mom says is generous since they're on Social Security."

"Not gonna win too many races with that thing." Matt examines the scraped-up frame and wheels, which are missing a few spokes. "Wrong kind of tires for racing."

But great for off-road.

"Like I said, I use it for hauling stuff." I want to

29

shove the pushy kid away from my bike, but I don't. Like it or not, I'm stuck here for a while.

"Yeah? Just what else you haul in that basket?"

Matt's eyes burn a hole in me. Mark saves me from a need to respond, his "excellent brain" asking the question that Lizzie had not finished earlier.

"But Dad, didn't you send money for a new bike—"

"Hush now, Mark," Lizzie interrupts.

"Bet his mama spent the money on dope," Matt whispers to his brothers.

"That's not true," I blurt out, wanting to set the record straight. "It wasn't like that at all. Mom was just helping out a friend. He told her that he'd give her a big tip if she'd pick something up for him. It was all a mistake."

Matt doesn't reply. Neither do FJ or Lizzie or the other brothers, so I don't say anything else.

What more is there to say? How can I explain to these strangers the way Mom's mind works? How she's always on the lookout for a "surefire deal" that's going to make us a fortune.

"This is gonna make us rich, Frankie Joe," she said when she invested the last of our savings in a deal that turned out to be crooked. We were supposed to get our money back when new investors signed up, plus make big interest.

Before that, she mortgaged our little house to buy a run-down shack to flip, just like she'd seen people do on TV. "Just a little paint on the walls and some petunias," she told me. She not only lost money on the house she flipped but our own house as well. We barely had enough money left to move into the trailer park.

Then a couple of years ago, she'd found the "real" surefire deal. I didn't find out exactly what that "real" surefire deal was until she was arrested for having a bag of dope in her purse. She'd gotten off light because it was her first offense and the dope was ditch marijuana—plants growing wild instead of imported from somewhere else.

But then this last summer, she decided to help that friend, picking up a package that came over the Mexican border so she could get a big tip. I mean, how was she to know what was in the package—and that the person she picked it up from was an undercover border cop? It *was* all a mistake.

I put my once-upon-a-time yellow bike into the metal rack holding four others so new the paint isn't even chipped. I eye those bikes a good long time, and then I hear another whisper, one that comes from inside my head.

What *did* happen to the money for a new bicycle?

Monday, September 21

7:45 A.M.

"Go right in, Mr. Huckaby." The Clearview School secretary for primary and middle school is a thin woman with long hair pulled into a knot that looks like a donut stuck on the back of her head. "The principal is waiting to see you. He got a fax from Laredo this morning."

The donut-headed woman raises her eyebrows when she mentions the fax. She motions me toward a row of chairs outside the principal's office, where I am to wait.

The principal wears a suit and tie, just like all the other principals I've known. The name painted on the glass door in blocky black letters says his name is MR. ROBERT ARNT.

"Don't forget that I'm just here temporarily," I whisper to FJ as he steps inside the principal's office. I put heavy emphasis on the word *temporarily,* which I'm taking a stronger liking to—thanks to four half brothers I didn't know I had, who are all so good at something.

32

I take a seat on one of the chairs that lets me see FJ and Mr. Arnt. I figure I won't be here but a couple of minutes. Then FJ will be on his way to inspect grain, and I'll follow the principal down the hall. Next I'll be made to stand in front of a class of giggly kids until the teacher assigns me a desk. That's the way it works in Laredo, and I figure it's the same here.

Please let there be a desk at the back of the room....

As the wall clock ticks off minutes, I notice the color of the tiles on the wall. Soybean green. No matter where I go, I can't get away from all that pukey green.

I decide to look inside the blue nylon backpack that Lizzie handed me this morning. It's an old one she recycled from one of her "weeds." Inside is a green notebook, the kind with enough dividers for six subjects, a pink rubber eraser, and an entire box of yellow number-two pencils, all sharpened.

I sigh and close the backpack. The clock ticks off more minutes. I see FJ and Mr. Arnt looking at some papers. When the principal gets up from his chair, I stand up, ready to be escorted to my room.

"Frankie Joe, you want to come in here, please?"

"In there?" The principal points me to a chair next to FJ, who's rubbing his mouth like there's bubble gum stuck on his lips.

"How are you doing, Frankie Joe?" The happy smile on Mr. Arnt's face does not match the unhappy look in his eyes.

"Um, is something wrong?"

"No—no. Just looking over your records. It seems you were well liked at your school, got along well with the other students and your teachers...." He clears his throat, and his smile disappears. "Well, it appears we *do* have somewhat of a problem." He shuffles the papers on his desk. "Given the information we just received from Laredo, we're not sure what to do with you—where to put you, I mean."

"Did you really go to school just eighty-two days last year?" FJ stops rubbing his mouth and looks at me. "Eighty-two days!"

"Maybe I better handle this," the principal says, giving FJ the fake-mouth smile. He turns his unsmiling eyes on me. "Is that a fact, Frankie Joe? Or are these records in error? If they're incorrect, I'll call down to Laredo and get it sorted out."

"Um, I don't know if they're correct or not. You see, I just go to school...temporarily." I hear FJ groan.

Principal Arnt clears his throat. "Well then, given your attendance record"—he pauses to pull a paper from the pile on his desk—"and your grade reports... I have no choice but to put you in...the fourth grade."

Fourth grade! I remember that Mark, the half brother with the "excellent brain" is in the fourth grade—and he's only old enough to be in the third!

Rubbing my mouth as though something sticky is on

34

it, I turn to FJ to make a last-ditch effort. "Remember, *Dad*, I'm, uh, I'm just here temporarily—"

"Be quiet," FJ snaps. He turns to the principal. "Let's reconsider this, Robert." When he calls the principal by his first name, I figure he's making a last-ditch effort of his own. "If you can't put him in the sixth, how about the fifth?"

Fifth—but I'm a sixth-grader!

"We have rules, FJ."

"I know you do, but I have rules, too—one of which is I expect my boys to be all they can be. All I'm asking is that you meet me half way. And I'll put him in the after-school program with the other boys."

"He's old enough to go home on his own—"

"I know that, but I figure he can do some catching up in there. It's done a world of good for the others." He looks at me. "And I will personally take charge of teaching him about responsibility." He puts heavy emphasis on the word *responsibility.*

The principal sighs. "All right then, we'll give it a try." Neither his mouth nor his eyes are smiling. "But mark my words, FJ. If he doesn't succeed there, I'll pull him out and put him where he belongs. Those are the rules."

"He *will* succeed," FJ says, looking at me again. "All my boys succeed. That's *my* rule."

"Okay then," Principal Arnt says. "I'll walk him

down to the classroom and let Mrs. Bixby know that The Great Escape is getting a new Huckaby."

Even though we won the battle, I feel like a loser.

I follow them out of the office. FJ leaves through the front door, and I follow the principal down the long soybean-green hallway. When he stops in front of one of the classrooms, I pause long enough to read the sign on the door: MRS. HOOPLE, FIFTH-GRADE ENGLISH.

Man-oh-man, I can't believe I have to do fifth grade again! As I enter the room, I look to see if there are any empty places at the back.

Cool. Four empty desks.

Then my eyes wander back to the front and come to rest on Matt, the half brother with the spark in his eye. Only now his eyes are round as saucers.

Yeah, I think. I didn't expect to see me standing here, either.

Mr. Arnt finishes saying what he needs to say to Mrs. Hoople and walks out the door, leaving me to my fate.

"Um, how about I take one of those desks at the back of the room?" I ask, putting a fake-mouth smile on my face. "You know, where it's not so crowded." But as soon as Mrs. Hoople looks at me, I know I'm sunk.

"Oh, I think not, Frankie Joe." Neither her mouth nor her eyes are smiling. "I think the best spot for you is next to my best student—the one who makes the honor roll every quarter and is fifth-grade representative to the Student Council. Sit yourself down right there next

36

to your brother. Mr. Arnt has assigned him to be your buddy. He'll show you the ropes."

I give Matt a sideways glance as I plop into the chair next to him.

"Kowabunga, dude," he whispers.

One corner of Matt's lip curls up in a grin. It's the kind of grin that says he's gonna show me the ropes, all right.

8:45 A.M.

There are four sentences in the paragraph. I'm on the third. "Ex…ex–tra…ex—tra-or—"

"It's *extraordinary*, retard," Matt whispers.

"Good grief," someone behind me says. "It's been five minutes, and he's still on the first paragraph!"

The bell rings, and I make for the door.

9:40 A.M.

I take a back seat in U.S. History, but Mrs. Carter, the teacher, immediately moves me to the front. She issues me a book that weighs at least ten pounds.

As it turns out, it's test day. We have to identify all the states and their capitals. I look at the blank map she lays on my desk, wishing I had paid more attention to the Triple A maps on the drive up from Texas.

I'm still working on my map when Mrs. Carter picks it up. She pauses long enough to make a *tsk-tsk* sound before moving on.

I stuff my book into my backpack five minutes before the bell rings, ready to make my getaway.

12:10 P.M.

The Science teacher's name is Mr. Burke. He points to a desk in the front row when I walk in and plops another ten-pound book on it. I get the feeling that he's been alerted that I'm coming. Of course, my desk is right next to Matt's.

Mr. Burke asks, "Who can tell me the freezing point of water?"

I struggle to understand the importance of frozen water. That's what refrigerators are for, right? Ice cubes.

Mr. Burke holds his hand flat like a crossing guard stopping traffic. Around the room, hands fly into the air, but no one speaks.

I get it. We're supposed to talk to the hand when we're called on. I don't raise my hand or open my mouth.

"Let's see..." Mr. Burke looks at his roll, the one he just added my name to. "Frankie Joe," he says, looking at me. "What's the freezing point of water?"

"Um, I didn't raise my hand." I hear giggles behind me.

Mr. Burke frowns and turns to Matt.

"Thirty-two degrees Fahrenheit or zero degrees Celsius." Matt grins at me. "And the boiling point is two hundred twelve degrees for Fahrenheit and one-hundred degrees for Celsius."

Showoff.

Mr. Burke nods, looking pleased. "Then what would be the degree of difference between boiling point and freezing point for each?" Hands fly as he raises the crossing-guard hand again.

"Okay, Mandy?" Mr. Burke calls on a short, blonde-haired girl sitting on the other side of me.

"A hundred and eighty for Fahrenheit...and, um, one hundred for Celsius."

"Right! Now for a test of your science *and* math skills. What would the Fahrenheit to Celsius ratio be?"

Ratio?

Only one hand goes up this time. Matt's. Even though it's not my hand, Mr. Burke looks at me again.

"Um," I say, and leave it at that. Mr. Burke frowns again, then gives Matt a nod.

"Well, there's a hundred-and-eighty degrees difference with Fahrenheit and one hundred for Celsius, so the ratio would be 1.8 to 1."

Huh?

"What would that look like?" Mr. Burke looks around the room. Matt's hand is the only one in the air again, so Mr. Burke points him to the white board.

Matt writes 1.8:1 on the board. "It's just comparing one thing to another," he says, "only in shorthand."

FJ probably taught him that, I think. His job is to analyze things.

Matt gives me the cocky grin again when he sits down.

Yeah, I get it. You're smart.

I'm relieved when the bell rings.

2:35 P.M.

In Math class, I mechanically take a front-row seat. The teacher, Mrs. Beard, nods her approval and hands me another huge book. She talks about estimating sums and how to check subtraction problems. Because we have a few minutes to kill just before class is over, she decides to do a quick review of multiplication tables, starting with the sevens.

I remember that Luke, the second-grader, knows how to count by sevens. I look at the clock. Five minutes to go.

"Volunteers?" she repeats, looking around the room.

Of course, Matt's hand shoots into the air. I cross my fingers and stare at my desk.

"Frankie *J-o-o-o-e*." Mrs. Beard lets the "o" in my name hang in the air like a balloon. "You start off. Do your sevens, please. One through fifteen."

3:30 P.M.

When the final bell rings, a rush of kids flies past me on their way home—but I stand outside the kindergarten room where the after-school program is held.

Lizzie explained this morning at breakfast that the program is for kids from kindergarten through fifth grade whose parents work. They don't want their kids staying alone until they get home, so they pay for them to stay at the school.

That doesn't make sense to me. I don't need a babysitter. I've stayed home alone for as long as I can remember, except when I was really little or nights when I stayed with Mrs. Jones.

A sign over the door says THE GREAT ESCAPE.

I wish! I hope there's a desk in a back corner.

I peek inside and see a woman with frizzy black hair and fidgety eyes in the middle of the room. She's telling other kids what to do and where to sit. Her arms never stop moving, reminding me of policemen in Mexico. They stand in the middle of intersections that have no stop signs, blowing their whistles and waving cars across the road.

Teachers begin entering the room. They hand the woman with waving arms and jumpy eyes homework assignments and spelling lists. My English, Math, History, and Science teachers are all there.

Someone bumps me from behind. "Boy, you're tall! How old are you?"

A short girl with a blonde ponytail is trying to get past me. I remember her from Science class. Her name is Mandy.

"Twelve," I mumble. "And I'm five foot nine."

"Wow, you're tall for twelve. What're you doing here? Oh, I know. You're that new kid. Boy, I'm glad you showed up. Used to be, I got kidded all the time 'cause

I'm so short. Now they can pick on you 'cause you're so tall."

Swell. Being a couple of inches taller than average is a reason to be picked on? Like I need another one. I miss my friends in Laredo. They like me the way I am.

"What's that mean?" I point to the sign over the door.

"The Great Escape?" She looks thoughtful. "Um, I think it means that we've been set free from school." She laughs. "I just realized what a joke that is!" Pony-tail swinging, Mandy troops past me to a desk at the back of the room. "Well, come on," she says, looking over her shoulder. "We've got to sign in."

I follow Mandy inside and write my name beneath hers on a sign-in sheet. "Is she tough?" I nod toward the frizzy-haired woman, who by now has talked with all the teachers.

"Mrs. Bixby? She's a real hard nose, but if you know how to work it, she's okay."

"What does that mean?"

"It means if she thinks you're cooperating with her, she eases up on you."

Mrs. Bixby beats a path to my side. "I've been expecting you." She holds her pointer finger under my nose. "Now listen close, here are my rules."

I sigh. Everyone in this alien universe has rules.

"First, you sign yourself in—but *never* sign yourself out. Only your parents or I can sign you out...." About a hundred rules later, she says, "Sit there!" She points me to a kindergartener-size chair at a table marked FIFTH GRADE. "I'll let you know the rest of the rules later. Now I must get the other students working on their assignments."

Rest of the rules? I try to repeat Mrs. Bixby's list of rules, but all I can remember is that I'm supposed to sit down. One thing is clear: With all these rules, there is no escape from The Great Escape.

I scrunch my taller-than-average twelve-year-old body into a dwarf-size chair, willing myself to disappear into the woodwork. Looking out the window, I see straight, neat rows of corn and soybeans growing in square- and rectangle-shape fields. I begin to daydream that I'm looking at the Chihuahua Desert and that Mr. O'Hare and I are hunting for space rocks. But Mrs. Bixby destroys that dream.

"Does everyone know Frankie Joe?" She scrunches into one of the miniature chairs at the fifth-grade table. "He's the oldest Huckaby now, which makes him Huckaby Number One." She turns to Matt. "That makes you Huckaby Number Two, Matthew."

Matt freezes in place—like he's just been tasered—and I have an awakening.

That's it! The reason he glares at me is because I've knocked him off the top of the heap. I don't get to enjoy the moment because Mrs. Bixby turns to me next.

"Frankie Joe, did you know that I quilt with Mrs.

Huckaby every Saturday afternoon? We've been best friends since first grade."

"No ma'am."

I can forget about disappearing into the woodwork.

"And don't forget"—Mrs. Bixby says, looking around the table—"our Quilt Circle is making a quilt for a Christmas raffle again this year. Our profits help fund The Great Escape." She smiles an extraordinarily wide smile at me. "Save your money so you can buy a ticket."

I put a fake smile on my face, wondering where she thinks I'm going to get money for a raffle ticket. In Laredo I work at Felipe's Corner Market on weekends, cleaning the stockroom. The owner likes me because I'm a hard worker and show up on time. He pays me in cash because I'm underage—ten dollars a day. In Laredo a lot of people get paid under the table—illegal aliens slip across the border all the time. But that job is gone, and I won't be getting tips from my neighbors at the Lone Star Trailer Park for running errands, either.

Besides, I think. Even if I had money, the last thing in the world I would buy is a raffle ticket for a quilt.

"Enough chitchat," Mrs. Bixby says. "Now to your studies. We need to practice spelling the names of the states." She glances my way. "Some of you didn't do so well on your test today." Paper and pencils and groans emerge around the table.

Cooperate, I think, remembering the advice Mandy

gave me. I take out my notebook and one of the yellow number-two pencils.

"Wis–con–sin," Mrs. Bixby says. She screws her face up in a very serious manner as she sounds out each syllable. I repeat the syllables silently and write each one down on my paper exactly the way I hear Mrs. Bixby say it.

She says the word again, more slowly. "Wis...con...sin." I notice she's watching to make sure that I'm writing. When everyone finishes, she asks, "Now who wants to make a sentence using the word *Wisconsin*?" Like magnets to metal, her eyes glom on to me.

"I'll go first," Matt says.

"Yeah, okay," I say, deciding it's all right with me if Matt wants to be number one.

"Now Matthew," Mrs. Bixby says, making a clucking noise with her tongue. "As our new student, Frankie Joe should have the honor of going first today."

Honor? I feel my face start to burn.

All eyes are locked on me. Matt's are glinting especially bright, and suddenly I want to show him that he isn't the only smart Huckaby sitting at the fifth-grade table. I rack my brain for something to say about Wisconsin.

"Wisconsin is called the Dairy State," I blurt out. "They make a lot of butter and cheese there."

A surprised look comes over Mrs. Bixby's face. "Why...that's a very good answer, Frankie Joe."

"Woo-hoo," another student down the table whispers. "The big slow kid did something right. First time today." Others start to laugh.

"Hush now," Mrs. Bixby tells them. She turns to me. "Now tell everyone how to spell Wisconsin, Frankie Joe."

I read aloud the letters I've written down, just as I heard her say them. "W–i–z . . . k–o–n . . . s–u–n."

Matt snorts. Mandy rolls her eyes. The other kids hoot. Mrs. Bixby makes a clucking noise.

And I feel my face go from burning to blazing.

4:45 P.M.

I trail behind the four legitimate Huckabys on the way home from school, which takes us right through downtown. We pass a grocery store and a hardware store, a post office, and a pizza place; a corner café, a gas station, and a gift shop.

Huckaby numbers two, three, four, and five don't seem to notice that Huckaby number one lags behind. They're having too good a time on their own, laughing and horsing around like brothers do. Real brothers.

I hate their legitimate guts. I want to get away from them, but I can't because I don't know the way. So I trudge on, carrying a backpack crammed full of ten-pound books. The Huckaby boys finished all their homework in The Great Escape, so they left their books in their lockers. I, on the other hand, will be working late into the night.

Finally I recognize where I am—almost to the Huckaby house. Turning the corner, I walk past an alley—and stop.

Why not? Lizzie won't be home from work, and I don't want to be alone with the mutant ninjas. I feel better the minute I take the first step.

I like alleys, especially alleys where wasteful people live. Wasteful people leave all kinds of treasures in their trash. I found the wrecked Rover Sport in an alley. And salvaged the basket off a girl's busted bike. Once I even found a toaster that still worked...sort of. With Mr. O'Hare's help, I fixed it, and Mrs. Jones bought it from me for two dollars. "Lot better than heating up the house with the stove just to toast some bread," she told me.

However, this particular alley does not look promising. It's the neatest alley I've ever walked through. The trash cans are lined up behind neat fences that border neat yards with trimmed grass and shrubs... except for one.

One place doesn't fit in with the rest. Yellow paint peels off the wood siding and crooked green shutters cling to loose nails. The foundation sags on one end, causing the house to tilt to one side. The grass has been mowed hit-or-miss, and hoes and rakes and garden tools are scattered around the yard.

I like this place. It's messy, like home.

A trash can sitting in back of the house looks like a

47

soda-pop can that a giant squeezed between its fingers. The can has no lid, so I look inside.

Empty. No treasure this afternoon. No looking for meteors from outer space. Just homework.

Life is very unfair. I take a kick at the beat-up garbage can; and because it's empty, it goes flying against a neighboring fence where it bounces and spins down the alley, rattling as it goes.

"Uh-oh," I whisper as I hear the squeak of a screen door. A woman comes outside, one hand shading her eyes so she can see better. The other hand holds a cane with a black rubber stop on the end.

"You there—you live around here?" she calls out.

"Yes ma'am."

Temporarily, I think. I set her trash can upright.

"Well, I don't recall seeing you before, and I know everyone in this town. I sell Nova, you see." She eyes me when I don't respond. "You know what that is? Nova?"

I shake my head no.

"Cosmetics! You know, makeup for women's faces? Lipstick, rouge, face powder, lotions. You never heard of Nova?"

I shake my head again.

"So you don't know me and I don't know you." She studies me like I'm a bug under a magnifying glass. "I'd say from looking, you'd be related to Frank Huckaby. That right?"

"Yes ma'am."

"Thought so. I've watched the kids in this town grow up, and you are the spitting image of Frank when he was a boy."

"I am?"

She nods. "A boy related to the Huckabys should know how to introduce himself properly."

"Oh. My name's Frankie Joe. Frankie Joe Huckaby."

"Frank's oldest boy?"

"Yes ma'am."

How did she know that?

"Well, my name's Peachcott. Miss Elsie Peachcott."

Elsie Peachcott is the kind of person you can't help but stare at, even though you know it's not polite. It's not because she's wrinkled and stooped like a troll that lives under a bridge. Or because she has black-licorice hair and eyebrows, and red-licorice circles painted on both cheeks. It's because of a large, muddy-brown spot on the side of her face. That spot draws my eyes like a magnet.

"What are you staring at?" Her watery blue eyes become slits. "Don't you know it's not polite to stare?"

"Nothin', I'm not looking at nothin'."

"Don't lie to me, boy. I've been the object of ridicule all my life. I can look in a person's eyes and tell when he's not being truthful. Now tell me, what are you looking at?"

"Your...face," I whisper.

"My face," she repeats. "My entire face? Or something on my face?"

49

I suck the spit from between my teeth. "Something on your face."

"You mean my birthmark? What, you've never seen a birthmark big as a silver dollar before?"

I shake my head no.

"Oh." She pauses. "Well, I suppose a person can't be held accountable for things they don't know." She leans closer. "Tell me, is it real obvious? Or just a little bit obvious?"

I'm not sure I want to get closer to the woman, but I do. I step through the gate and walk half way to the porch. But even then, I can't see the spot clearly because something has been smeared on top of it.

"I can't tell 'cause there's something chalky-looking on it."

Without warning, Elsie Peachcott pounds her cane on the porch. "Blast it all, I still don't have it right!" Looking around, she lowers her voice. "I been working on a makeup formula that will blend into whatever you skin tone is—including birthmarks. You see, Nova's interested in buying it if I can get it right." She gives me a raised-eyebrow look. "And you know what that means?"

"Um...what?"

"It means I can retire, live the good life!" She shakes her head. "Nothing else to do, I suppose, but make another batch." She studies me some more. "So you've come home to roost, have you, Frankie Joe Huckaby?"

"Home to roost?"

"Come up here on this stoop," she says, talking in a raspy whisper. "Can't you see that I'm crippled up and it's hard for me to come down there?"

"I got to go home—"

"Are you sassing your elders?"

"No ma'am."

"Well then, get on up here! Can't be standing in the yard yelling our business at one another. Be all over this one-horse town before you can blink. People get in your business here. You don't know that now, you'll learn it quick enough." She pounds her chest with her free hand. "Got to hold your business close to your chest."

"Yes ma'am, I learned that already."

"All right then. We'll have a cookie, and you can tell me how you come to be back here."

5:05 P.M.

"Why did you say . . . 'back here'?"

I shuffle into the kitchen behind Miss Peachcott—if you can call the room where I'm standing a kitchen. It's more like a mad scientist's laboratory. Beakers and funnels and test tubes take the place of mixing bowls and measuring spoons and baking pans. Jars and bottles of different-color powders and liquids clutter the countertops. Stacks of boxes in all the corners have pink labels marked NOVA stuck on their sides.

"Help yourself to a cookie," she says, putting tubes

and jars into a pink sack. "I have to make deliveries after I finish up these orders. This one's for the widow, Mrs. Brown."

She stops working to look at me. "There's one for the books. Woman was skinny as a beanpole before her husband died. Now he's passed over, she's fattened up like a pig." She rolls the top down on the bag and picks up another one.

I open cupboard doors, looking for cookies. More Nova stuff.

She begins to put things into the second bag. "This order's for *Miz* Bloom, that divorcee that's tryin' to look half her age. Can always tell a divorcee because she refers to herself as *Miz*. Not even I can help that one— and I have helped many a woman look half her age."

I open the refrigerator. No cookies.

"And this order's for that newlywed, Mrs. Barnes— pregnant already."

Oven. I take a chance.

Woo-hoo. I pull out a package of Oreos and help myself to two. Because the table and chairs are stacked with boxes, I stand in the middle of the floor.

"You said something before," Miss Peachcott says, turning to look at me. "Did you ask a question?"

I swallow the last of the cookie in a gulp. " 'Back here,' " I say, spewing crumbs across the room. "Outside there, you said something about me being 'back here.' "

"Oh, yes. You're supposed to tell me what you're doing back here again."

"Well," I say slowly, "I didn't know I was here before."

Miss Peachcott's eyes go round. "You don't know that you were born here?"

"I was born in Clearview?" I feel *my* eyes go round.

In a blink, Miss Peachcott leaves off sacking up cosmetics and clears a space at the table.

"My goodness, child, I can't believe she never told you where you were born. Why, your daddy worried about you something awful after you left. Of course, I've known him since he was knee high to a grasshopper. His mama was one of my first customers—encouraged me to go into business on my own." She pauses. "Maybe that's why FJ confided things like that to me. I was kind of a second mother to him."

She pushes her glasses up on her nose and motions me to sit down. "Well, you see, it was this way...."

5:15 P.M.

"I suppose Martha Jane came by her jackrabbit ways natural enough," Miss Peachcott says.

Martha Jane is Mom's name, only it's not what she wants to be called. "Marti doesn't sound so old-fashioned," she once told me. "Know what I mean, kiddo?"

"And Mom was born here, too—like me?"

"Born and reared right here. Martha Jane Elliott."

Miss Peachcott shoves the sack of cookies toward me. "Your grandparents worked at a dairy—did the milking, cleaned the milk house. Martha Jane had to help, too. Hard life. Have to milk twice a day, you know. Morning and night." She hesitates. "And then both your grandparents got killed in an accident, right out there on the road into town. Hit by a grain truck. But I guess she told you that."

I shake my head no. Mom never told me that. She never told me much of anything.

"Anyway, Martha Jane went to live with the only family she had left. Your aunt Geraldine—only she preferred to be called Gerry."

Miss Peachcott goes *humph*.

I go *hmmm*, thinking about the way Mom changed her name to Marti.

"Geraldine was a wild sort," Miss Peachcott continues. "Lived downtown in one of the upstairs apartments that looked out over the town square." Her eyes twinkle. "Back then Clearview wasn't such a one-horse town. Fresh-air movies on the square in the summer. Even had a bowling alley and a baseball team! You like baseball?"

I hear the question, but my mind is on something else. "What do you mean, 'wild sort'?"

"Irresponsible! Liked to go out partying. Dance and live it up. She worked odd jobs—waitressed here and there, barhopped at some of the taverns. Clearview wasn't big enough for her; she was always chasing rain-bows." She pushes her glasses up on her nose and eyes me. "You know what that means? Chasing rainbows?"

"She, uh, she wanted to make it big?"

"Exactly. Well anyway, Geraldine took off with a man passing through town." She shakes her head. "Never heard from her again."

"She took off! But what about Mom?"

"Well," she says, pausing. "Of course, Martha Jane was the impressionable sort. What high school girl isn't? She liked living with her aunt Geraldine, that's for sure. And she was just as eager to rid herself of this one-horse town. Anyway, after she was left high and dry, she was taken in by a widow lady. Good soul, but strict. The two didn't hit it off."

She pauses again. "Then *you* happened. Don't know why Frank and Martha Jane didn't marry up, but I figure it was Martha Jane's idea to leave town. When she turned eighteen, she came into a little money—insurance settlement from her folks' accident. Said she was going to use it for a stake somewhere else." She looks at me. "Don't know what she did with the money or where she ended up."

"Mom bought us a house in Laredo...but she had to sell it."

"In Texas? My, my. Well, all I know is, we never heard from her again."

"Like Aunt Geraldine."

55

"Just so."

I don't know whether I feel better or worse.

Miss Peachcott straightens her back. "Now what are you doing back here, Frankie Joe Huckaby? And what's that jackrabbit mother of yours been up to all these years?"

I chew a cookie slowly, wondering what I should do. I like this little woman; she reminds me of my friends at the trailer park. But she cautioned me to keep my business close to my chest—and all she's done is talk about other people.

I think about the kids in the after-school program calling me "the big slow kid." If word got out about Mom, would they call her names, too?

I can't let that happen.

"I'm just here temporarily," I say, picking up my backpack. "Only a few months."

"Stop right there, buster." Miss Peachcott grabs me by the sleeve. "What's the rest of it? Now you look me in the eye and tell me what your mother's been up to down there in Texas all this time."

I turn away from the woman who can look into a person's eyes and tell when he's lying. "Stuff," I say as I push through the screen door. "Just...stuff."

That's what my mouth says. But in my mind, I hear a voice say, "Chasing rainbows; she's been chasing rainbows."

"How did your first day at school go, Frankie Joe?" Lizzie dishes me up a big plate of mashed potatoes and corned beef and cabbage.

"All right," I say, ignoring the sputtering giggles coming from Matt. Following in his footsteps, Mark, Luke, and Little Johnny start giggling, too.

He's told them how dumb I am.

"So...you have any problems?" FJ looks at me, then eyes the other boys. They lower their heads and chow down like a herd of wild, dark-eyed pigs called *javelina* that live in the Chihuahua Desert.

I hate them all. Every last one of them.

"No sir," I say, biting my tongue. "No problems."

More sputtering from Matt.

"I got lots of homework," I say as soon as supper is over. I get up from chair and head for the stairs."

"Hold up," FJ says, stopping me. "We have some unfinished business. Remember?"

I don't.

"Follow me," he says. In the living room, he pulls a dictionary from the bookshelf. "Look up the word *responsibility.*"

I remember. In the principal's office that morning, FJ swore he would personally teach me about responsibility. I thumb through the dictionary as my mutant ninja posse troops into the room.

"Here it is," I say, hoping he doesn't ask me to read it aloud.

"Good," he says, checking the dictionary entry. "Now write it down." He points me to his desk and fishes a pencil and index card out of a drawer. Huckabys numbers two, three, four, and five sit down on the sofa to watch.

What is this?

"Don't you boys have homework to do?" FJ asks, seeming to read my mind. In unison they shake their heads no. "Then go to your rooms and play games."

"We got all our homework done," Matt says, appointing himself spokesperson for the group. "We've earned the right to watch TV."

"Later." FJ points at the stairs. "Frankie Joe and I need some time alone. You'll have to find other things to do."

Matt glares at me. The other Huckaby boys whine, but they go upstairs.

I write the definition down as FJ watches.

re-spon-si-bil-i-ty \ *noun*:   **1** : the quality or state of being responsible: as **a** : moral, legal, or mental accountability **b** : RELIABILITY, TRUSTWOR-THINESS   **2** : something for which one is responsible : BURDEN

Burden. You can say that again! I hand the completed card to FJ.

"Your penmanship could use some work, too," he says, reading the definition. "I'll have Lizzie talk to Mrs. Bixby."

Swell.

"I want you to put this on the wall above your desk," he says, handing me the index card, "and read it every day."

Taking the card, I head for the stairs.

"I'm not finished," FJ says. "I also expect a report every Sunday showing what you've done to satisfy that definition."

"A report?"

"Homework counts...and your chores." He takes a paper from his pocket. "On my lunch hour, I made out this chore schedule. Five boys, five days worth of chores. In addition to taking care of your own room and hauling down your laundry, there's helping with meals and cleaning up afterward. On weekends you'll be expected to help with outside work." He hands me the list and nods toward the stairs. "Now get to that homework. Lights out at ten—house rule."

Another rule. As I head upstairs with my definition and chore list, FJ stops me again.

What now—more rules?

"When you're done with your homework," he says, "come on down and watch TV with the others."

"Thanks, but I got a ton of it." I can't think of anything I'd rather *not* do than spend the evening with the legitimate Huckabys. I take the steps two at a time, for the first time in my life glad for homework.

Taping the definition and chore list to the wall above my desk, I spend the rest of the evening on English and Math, History and Science. I try to push the echo of the half brothers' sputtering giggles out of my head, but it stays there in the background.

At ten o'clock when I finally close the books and crawl into the squeaky old bed, I'm thinking just one thing.

Soon as I can, I'm gonna rid myself of this one-horse town...just like Mom did.

Sunday, September 27

4:20 P.M.

Lizzie walks into the kitchen as I'm getting ready to take out the trash—one of my chores today. Tonight I have to hand in my first Responsibility Report.

Since I know how to multiply by four, I figure how many reports I have to do in the ten months I'll be there. Four weeks in a month times ten months—

Forty reports!

I look over the list of chores and homework. One more chore will fill out a full page of notebook paper. I'm determined to fill in that last line, and this chore will do it.

"My, aren't you the busy one," Lizzie says, smiling her big smile. She's barely hung up her jacket when there's a knock on the door.

I'm slow recognizing the munchkin in the Girl Scout uniform that she invites inside. Mandy. A miserable-looking Mandy.

"*Puh-leeze*, Mrs. Huckaby," she says. "*Puh-leeze* buy

a box of cookies from me. I'll do anything for you if you do." She looks around the kitchen. "I'll sweep the floor...or wash the dishes or"—she jerks the trash bag out of my hand—"I'll take out the trash."

"No way!" I take the trash bag away from Mandy. She's not about to cheat me out of a full page.

When she reaches for it again, I hold it over her head. She jumps for it like she's on a trampoline.

"Stop it, you two." Lizzie places her hands on her hips, frowning, and then turns to Mandy. "Of course, I'll buy a box, Mandy. Now why the long face?"

Mandy collapses onto a kitchen chair. "Oh thank you thank you, Mrs. Huckaby." She hands Lizzie the order form for cookies. "What's wrong is I wasn't born an only child. Do you know how hard it is to sell cookies when you have two older sisters who are Girl Scouts, too? My sisters have regular customers who buy from them every year. The youngest kid in the family doesn't stand a chance!"

Lizzie hands me the cookie list. "Pick out something, Frankie Joe. *Two* somethings."

All right. A list to look at that doesn't involve work. I sit down at the table next to Mandy.

Lizzie pulls some sodas out of the refrigerator and sits down at the table across from us. "You're preaching to the choir, Mandy." She pushes the sodas toward Mandy and me. "I was the youngest child in my family— and it was a family of seven!"

"Oh good grief how did you stand it?"

Mandy's running her words together like she's on a sugar high.

"It wasn't easy," Lizzie says, grinning. "But having sisters—and brothers—is a good thing." She looks at me. "Right, Frankie Joe?"

"Um, sure."

Liar, liar, pants on fire....

Concentrating on the cookie list, I decide on mint and peanut-butter cookies, and hand the form to Mandy.

She downs the last of her soda and gets up to leave. "Thanks," she tells Lizzie. "You're just the greatest."

"I hope things start to look up for you." Lizzie walks Mandy to the back door.

"Well actually, I guess it already has," Mandy rattles on. "At least I'm not the oddball at school now that Frankie Joe's here."

Lizzie puts her hand on Mandy's shoulder, stopping her from leaving. "What do you mean, 'oddball'?"

Don't, I eye-telegraph Mandy. But she's still on her high.

"Well you see, I got teased a lot 'cause I was she shortest kid in the class. You know, the *oddball*. Now Frankie Joe's the oddball 'cause he's the tallest." She laughs. "He's a *double* oddball."

I send Mandy the eye-telegraph again. She gets it this time.

Lizzie looks between Mandy and me, and waits.

Mandy's mouth looks like it's been glued shut with super glue.

"It's not a big deal," I mumble. "Besides, I just made a new friend who's an oddball, and she doesn't let it bother her."

Lizzie frowns. "Who are you talking about, Frankie Joe?"

"Miss. Peachcott—"

"Miss Peachcott! Ohmigosh, she's got this...*thing* on her face—"

"Mandy!" Lizzie gives her a look.

Mandy seals her lips tight again.

"So what? You're short, I'm tall, and she's got a birthmark."

"There you go," Lizzie says, smiling again. "And Elsie doesn't let a birthmark get in the way of running a successful business. She's a fine role model for both of you." She opens the door and lets Mandy out. "So don't let anything stand in your way just because you're short"—she glances my way—"or tall."

As Mandy leaves, I pick up the trash bag for the second time. I plan to strangle Mandy on the way to the garbage can for the "double oddball" crack.

"Not so fast," Lizzie says. "What did Mandy mean, 'double oddball'?"

Too late.

"Um..." I hesitate too long.

"Spit it out, Frankie Joe, or I'll call the principal."

"I'm slow. They call me names 'cause I'm slow."

"Names." She frowns. "Who's calling you names?"

"I'd, uh, I'd rather not say."

She probably wouldn't believe me, if I told her.

"O-kay." She stretches the word out like it's a rubber band. "Then why do they think you're slow?"

" 'Cause I read slow and can't spell."

For beginners....

Lizzie starts blinking fast. "Well, I can't fix 'tall' but maybe I can help fix 'slow.' Come with me."

I set the trash bag down again and follow Lizzie. When we reach the front room, she hands me the dictionary from the bookshelf.

"This is yours now. Take it to your room so that it's handy when you need it. The boys have one in each of their bedrooms, and it's only fair that you do, too."

Great.

"Thanks," I say. I start for the stairs to put away the dictionary, but Lizzie stops me again.

"My goodness, I've helped four boys with homework for years. I'll just start helping you, too."

I'm gonna kill Mandy.

"*And* I'll talk to Mrs. Bixby. Did you know she's a good friend of mine? I know she won't mind putting in some extra time with you—maybe on Saturdays when we quilt."

All I wanted to do was finish my Responsibility Report! I put a fake-mouth smile on my face.

Lizzie smiles, too. "No need to thank me, Frankie Joe. That's what family's are for...." Her voice trails off, and her eyes start blinking again.

Uh-oh.

Quickly Lizzie writes something down on an index card. "Here," she says. "This can be the first word you look up in your very own dictionary."

I look at the word. *Home?*

"I don't think a one of us ever welcomed you to our home, Frankie Joe. It's high time we did. I want you to feel comfortable here—comfortable enough to tell us when something's not going good. Okay?"

I stretch the fake-mouth smile wider.

"Now you better get that trash out before Frank gets back. Might as well get one more thing on your Responsibility Report before you turn it in. Right?"

That was the idea.

5:16 P.M.

As I dump the trash, I wonder if Mandy's still selling cookies. Figuring she hasn't gotten far, I go in search of her. I stop at the end of the alley, look both ways, and spot a Girl Scout uniform a block away. I head toward her, but stop when I hear a familiar voice behind me.

"What'cha doin', Frankie Joe? Dumpster diving?" Matt's biking with some of our classmates. Laughing, he tells the others where I got my bike.

I leave them hooting and catch up with Mandy, who's still long-faced.

"Still no luck, huh?" Her order form hasn't gotten any fuller.

"Not much," she says. "Look, I didn't mean to cause you any grief back there."

"What's a little more grief." When she looks at me funny, I say, "Forget it. Come with me. I got an idea."

"Where we goin'?"

"You'll see." A few minutes later, I walk her up the steps to Miss Peachcott's back door.

Mandy hesitates. "But this is—"

"Yeah, the third oddball." I knock on the door.

"Frankie Joe! I was hoping you'd stop by." Miss Peachcott has been experimenting again. The spot on her face looks radioactive.

"This is Mandy. She's selling Girl Scout cookies." I shove Mandy forward. "I ate most of your cookies when I was here last time. And since you're so busy with your *project*"—I raise my eyebrows meaningfully when I say "project"—"I thought you might want to shop at home."

"Well now, isn't that clever of you." Miss Peachcott raises her eyebrows, too.

Mandy's frozen, so I take the order form from her hand and give it to Miss Peachcott.

"Why don't I just take a box of each," she says, making checkmarks across the page. "They all look too good to pass up." She returns the form to Mandy and gives me another raised-eyebrow look. "Now I must get back to my...*project*."

After saying good-bye to Miss Peachcott, I walk Mandy to the end of the alley.

"Gee thanks, Frankie Joe." Mandy stares at her order form, looking stunned. "This is absolutely great— *super* great." She looks at me. "Any time I can help you out—"

"Thanks," I say, walking away quickly, "but I've got all the help I can stand."

8:22 P.M.

home \ *noun:* **1 a :**   one's place of residence : DOMICILE **b :** HOUSE   **2 :** the social unit formed by a family living together   **3 a :** a familiar or usual setting : congenial environment; *also :* the focus of one's domestic attention [*home* is where the heart is]

   b. HABITAT   **4 a :** a place of origin [salmon returning to their *home* to spawn]; *also :* one's own country [having troubles at *home* and abroad] **b :** HEADQUARTERS   **5 :** an establishment providing care for people with special needs [*homes* for the elderly] [a *home* for unwed mothers]

Reading the definition a second time, I decide I like it. Grabbing a pencil, I rewrite the definition and tape it next to the *responsibility* card on the wall.

HOME—

One's place of residence **Lone Star Trailer
    Park**

The social unit formed by a family living
    together **Lone Star Trailer Park**

A familiar or usual setting : congenial
    environment **Lone Star Trailer Park**

Where the heart is **Lone Star Trailer Park**

One's own country **Lone Star Trailer Park**

An establishment providing care for the elderly
    Lone Star Trailer Park

An establishment providing care for unwed
    mothers **Lone Star Trailer Park**

I slide the dictionary into the bookshelf next to my
mementos from Mrs. Jones and Mr. O'Hare and Mr.
Lopez. Missing them, I start to wonder what they did
today. But I already know.

Mr. O'Hare would have gone hunting space rocks…
without me. The last time we went out together, he
packed peanut-butter-and-jelly sandwiches and bottles
of water for when we got tired. We sat in the shade of
a big red boulder and some mesquite bushes, and fed
crumbs to a desert horned lizard.

And Mr. Lopez would have painted a house. He works
every day so he can send money to his family in Mexico.
I wonder what color he created for today's house. He let
me name the last batch he created, which looked like

caramel sauce for ice cream. He came up with all kinds of names, but he liked mine best. Butter-Brickle Yellow.

It's Sunday, the day after the last Saturday of the month, so Mrs. Jones would have gone to the library to pick up "retired" books from her friend. Maybe she brought home another adventure book, like *Treasure Island* and *Kidnapped*. I bet she waits until I get home so we can read it together. I wish I were there to help her put the new books on her shelves. She likes me to help her because sometimes she has to move a whole shelf of books, which is a lot of work. Last time we shelved books, she fixed us ice cream sundaes as a reward.

I wish I were there with them now. Most of all, I wish I was home with Mom. She liked to do fun things on Sundays, like go to the movies. Instead of fixing lunch, she'd say, "What'll it be, kiddo? Popcorn or pretzels with mustard?" Then we'd each get something different at the movie and share with each other.

I read the definition for *home* one more time, then pull on my pajamas and turn back the covers. *I'll read this definition every day, too*, I think as I switch off the light. *Maybe twice a day.*

Friday, October 2

5:48 P.M.

Squeezing the last plate and bowl into the dishwasher, I close the door and push the START button. I can hear the half brothers in the front room, talking loud. Friday nights are movie nights, which means arguments. What to have for snacks? Who's going to sit where? Which movie to watch?

None of which involves me. What involves me is my Responsibility Report. It's due on Sunday. I put *dishes* on the list and look it over. Another page is filling up fast. My second week is almost over.

Only two weeks? It seems like two years.

All four brothers burst into the kitchen. "It's gonna be popcorn," Matt says, scrounging in the pantry for microwave popcorn.

"Why do you always get to choose?" Little Johnny's bottom lip droops, and his eyes look wet.

Lizzie walks into the kitchen. "What's all the noise about?"

"Nothing," Matt says. "I got it under control." He shuts the door on the microwave and punches in three minutes.

"But Mark and me wanted to make instant pudding," Johnny says. "Why does Matt always get what he wants?"

" 'Cause he's a control freak," Mark says.

Right on, Mark! Deciding to leave the noisy kitchen to Lizzie, I head for the door.

"Hold up, Frankie Joe." She points me and the other boys to the kitchen table. We sit down and listen to popcorn *ping!* in the microwave. Lizzie removes the bag and dumps it into a bowl, then sits down, too.

She stares into space awhile, looking thoughtful, then turns to me. "Did I ever tell you that I came from a family of seven, Frankie Joe?"

"Yes ma'am. That night Mandy came by. You said you were the youngest."

"That's right," she says, munching on popcorn. "There was my mom and dad and two brothers and two sisters. I was the baby."

The brothers dip into the popcorn bowl, looking bored. I stare at Lizzie, wondering if she's through talking to me. She's not.

"You know what's so nice about *odd*-numbered families?" she asks me, her eyes twinkling.

I get it. *Odd*ball...*odd*-numbered families.

"No ma'am," I say.

"There's always a tiebreaker!" She gives me her big smile and then looks around the table at her "weeds." "Whenever there was an argument among us five kids, we'd take a vote. And because there was an odd number, there was never a tie."

She turns to me again. "So you see, seven is the perfect number. And *you* made that happen, Frankie Joe. See what a nice addition you are to our family?"

I don't like being lumped with the "weeds." From the look on his face, Matt doesn't like it, either. Figuring Lizzie doesn't really expect me to answer, I don't. Sure enough, she keeps on talking.

"So new rule! Now that we have enough in the family to break a tie, I don't want to hear any more arguments." She marches her eyes around the table. "Understood?"

Hearing a chorus of "yes ma'ams," she smiles, then leaves the room.

Great. I attempt another escape.

"Hold up, Trailer Trash." Matt's eyes are sparking like hot coals. "You're not part of this family. *Understood?* So keep your nose out of our business!"

Don't you mean *your* business, Control Freak?

"No problem," I say, and walk out the back door.

6:17 P.M.

I wheel my Rover Sport off the front porch and look for Mandy. At school today, she said that she was going

73

out to sell cookies after supper. Wondering how she's doing, I make a fast run around the neighborhood. I've learned my way around Clearview pretty fast because it isn't that big. I've ridden across rock outcroppings in the Chihuahua Desert that are bigger.

I figure Mandy's looking for new territory. Sure enough, I find her in front of the pizza place downtown, hawking cookies to those going in for the Friday-night two-for-one special.

"Just think," she's telling a woman as I pull up. "If you keep boxes of cookies in your freezer, you'll have dessert ready on Friday nights. Pizza and cookies—instant supper!"

Not bad, I think. She's pretty good at selling things. The woman buys it, too.

When we're alone, I ask, "How many did she take?"

"Four! Does your mom want to buy some more cookies, too?"

"Lizzie's not my mom," I snap. Mandy looks surprised, so I don't say anything for a few seconds. Then I start thinking about Friday-night movies and arguments over treats. "But she might buy some more. Mark and Johnny are getting tired of popcorn."

"Cool! I'll mention that when I talk to her."

"Matt usually makes the call on treats, though."

"I don't know how you stand living with Matt Huckaby," she says, frowning. "He's so full of himself."

"Yeah. Um, it's probably better you don't mention

74

my name if he's there when you talk to Lizzie." I hesitate. "And that's not why I'm here."

"Oh? Then why?"

All at once, I feel foolish.

"Hurry, Frankie Joe. Another car's pulling up—more customers."

"It's about tiebreakers," I blurt out. "The thing about odd-numbered families is there's always a tiebreaker. You got three kids in your family—an odd number. Maybe you can use that with your older sisters. You know, when they get pushy."

"What a great idea!"

"Run it by your folks first," I tell her. "Get them on your side." Seeing a man and woman walking up, I say, "Gotta go."

"Thanks, *Oddball*," Mandy yells as I wheel off. I can still hear her laughing when I round the corner.

I know she didn't mean anything bad. Still, the name stings.

Saturday, October 3

8:10 A.M.

The water feels like needles hitting my skin. I haven't had a hot shower since I arrived. Two weeks of cold showers. Every...Single...Day.

The half brothers have a pecking order for shower-taking. Which means Matt is always first, followed by Mark, Luke, and Little Johnny. Then me. Bottom of the pecking order. By the time I get the shower, the hot water is gone. Down-to-the-last-drop gone.

My teeth are chattering when I get out. I'm too cold to towel-off good, so my shorts stick to my butt when I pull them up.

Who's gonna know?

I pull my jeans over damp shorts, and then a sweatshirt over my head and socks on my feet. Glancing in the mirror, I notice my lips are blue. I brush my teeth fast, so they won't crack from the icy water. In Laredo I don't have to worry about a cold butt and frozen teeth. With just Mom and me, we never run out of hot water.

I gather my wet towel and pajamas and add them to pile of dirty laundry I left in the hallway. Lizzie does the bedding on Saturdays, and I have to haul my other things down, too. I clump downstairs, loaded down with cold-wet-stinky clothes.

"Don't have to deal with cold, damp clothes in Texas, either," I mutter, pulling damp shorts out of my crotch. Texas is so hot, clothes dry fast.

But I did get stinky, I remember. Off-road biking in the Chihuahua Desert is a dirty business. But so much fun.

When I walk into the kitchen, Lizzie asks, "Did you sleep late?"

"No ma'am. I just had my turn in the shower. I'm always last." I drop my cold-wet-stinky clothes off in the laundry room and sit down.

Huckaby Numbers Two, Three, and Four are already at the table. Number Five is sitting on a stool next to Lizzie. A giant box of Bisquick, a carton of eggs, and a gallon of milk sit on the counter. She's helping Johnny measure ingredients into a bowl. FJ is missing, so I figure he had an early-morning appointment with a farmer.

Scratch that, I think, seeing a place has been set at the table for him, too. I wonder where he is.

"Okay, Frankie Joe, let's get started," Lizzie says. "Wy–o–ming." She's looking at my spelling list.

Can't a kid catch a break around here? It's Saturday!

I don't answer right away. My mind is still on Texas. Quickly I calculate how much longer I have to stay in Illinois. It's the first week of October, and Mom gets out of jail in mid-July. Only nine-and-a-half months to go.

Only nine-and-a-half months. . . .

"Wy–o–ming," Lizzie repeats slowly. She gives me a cautious look. "Remember what we talked about with those vowels. Sometimes they can get tricky."

Since Mandy's Girl-Scout-cookie visit, Lizzie has been quizzing me on my spelling words every morning. Along with that came tutoring on things such as "silent vowels" and "sound-alike letters" and rules like "*i* before *e* except after *c*." It's enough to put my mind in a fog.

"Wy–o–ming," I repeat. I study the patterns on the wallpaper, wishing the pictures were of cactus and sagebrush instead of red and green apples. Breathing deep, I begin. "W–i—" I stop, hearing Lizzie catch her breath. "Um, I mean, W–Y–o–m–i–n–g."

"Right," she laughs. "One hundred percent right."

"Wow, that was a tough one," Little Johnny says as he stirs blueberries into pancake batter. Flour dusts his face, and milk dribbles down the front of his shirt. He's happy because he got to choose what we have for breakfast this morning.

"That's not tough," Matt snorts. "I can spell it easy. I can spell all the states *and* the state capitals."

If I had food in my stomach, I'd throw up.

"Well that's good," Lizzie says, ladling pancake batter onto a griddle. "But right now, I want to talk about whose turn it is to choose breakfast next Saturday."

Without hesitating, Matt speaks up. "Johnny had his turn today, so it's my turn next."

"Nuh-unh," Luke says, pushing his glasses up his nose. "Now there's five of us—" His face turns as red as one of the apples on the wallpaper. "What I mean is, uh…"

"What he means," Lizzie says, dishing pancakes onto plates, "is a rotation system's the way we've always done things. Oldest down to the youngest. And I don't see any reason not to continue that way." She pauses to look at Matt. "And *that* means it's Frankie Joe's turn to pick a favorite food for next Saturday's breakfast."

I sit silent as a rock. I don't want a turn. A turn would just make things worse for me. Huckaby Number Two would make sure of that.

"And that's not all," Lizzie says. "From now on, the same rotation system goes for the shower. I know it's a lot, having all of you take your showers in the morning. But I have to do laundry in the evening—and run the dishwasher, too—which only leaves enough hot water for your father and me to bathe in the evenings. So we're going to a rotation system."

"But I'm the oldest—the *real* oldest," Matt protests. "And besides, I have to be to school earlier than the others 'cause I'm the fifth-grade representative on the Student Council."

"Does that mean I don't have to shower last no more?" Johnny screws up his face like he's thinking hard about something. "Except now that Frankie Joe's here, he showers last. It's not fun 'cause Matt hogs the hot water so there's not enough for all of us. I know 'cause I was always last till Frankie Joe got here."

"Is that right?" Lizzie looks at Matt, her eyebrows raised. "Well, no more being last all the time—for *any* of you. You'll take turns. And you're limited to two minutes each, no more."

"Cool," Mark says as he butters his pancake. "I hated lukewarm showers all the time."

As he reaches for the syrup bottle, Luke says, "Yeah, double cool! I hated chilly showers all the time, too."

There are daggers in the look Matt gives me.

"Now," Lizzie says, looking at me. "What do you want for your special breakfast next Saturday, Frankie Joe?"

"Something tells me he'd like burritos." FJ stands at the back door, holding a bunch of letters in one hand.

He must have been at the post office. I didn't hear him come in and don't know how long he's been standing there. But the smile he gives Lizzie says that he's heard all her announcements.

"Well then"—Lizzie returns his smile—"burritos it is!"

"What's a 'bri–to'?" Mark asks, looking skeptical. His "excellent brain" obviously doesn't include the word in its vocabulary.

"It's made from corn and beans," I say.

"Oh," Mark says, helping himself to another pancake. "Cool!"

"And it's bur–ri–to," I say. "B–u–r–r–i–t–o."

9:00 A.M.

FJ follows me to the front room after breakfast. "Here you go, Frankie Joe." He hands me a letter. "This came for you today."

My heart jumps when I look at the returning address on the envelope. It says "Webb County Texas Jail." Racing upstairs I sit down at my desk and open the envelope carefully so I don't tear the letter inside. I'm disappointed when I see there's only one page.

Can't be much to write about when you're locked up, I think. I would know.

My hands begin to shake when I see Mom's handwriting. I try to read slow, but I can't. It's like she's right there, talking to me.

Hi Kiddo!

How are things there in Dullsville, Sillynois? (ha-ha) Did you ever see so much corn in your life?

Jail's OK I guess. The food's soso and the bunk

81

could be softer. The mattress is thin as a pancake. Not much privacy ether. Guards are everwhere you look; they stick their nose in everthing. But I've met some neat gals; we play cards and talk to pass the time. A couple of them are talking about going into business together and asked me if I would be interested. I told them I might be.

I can have visitors on Tuesdays. That jerk Ricky came to see me last week. He's that friend I told you about. You know, the one that set up that deal that went bad. He apologized for getting me in trouble, swore he thought it was on the up-and-up. I'm still mad at him for not coming forward when I got arrested. He told me he'd been checking out a deal in Nevada and said he'd make it up to me. I'm planning on talking to a lawyer soon to see if I can get a new hearing. Keep your fingers crossed!!!

Hey look, kiddo, I'm real sorry about this mess. I was just trying to make a few bucks. I'll be out of this joint before you know it.

I'm not much of a writer, but that doesn't mean I'm not thinking of you. I can hardly wait to see you. Love ya loads!

Marti

XOXOXO

I read the letter a second and third time, and then read my favorite parts again.

I'm planning on talking to a lawyer soon to see if I can get a new hearing....

I wonder how long that will take. My heart pounds like a drum. Maybe she'll get out early!

Keep your fingers crossed!!!

"You can bet on it, Mom."

I can hardly wait to see you....

"Me too—"

Hearing a creak, I turn toward the stairs. It's FJ.

"Lizzie thought you might want to write to your mom." He lays a stack of envelopes and a book of stamps on my desk. "You got paper?"

"Yes sir." I indicate the open notebook on my desk. "Thanks."

"Thank Lizzie. It was her idea. I'll take your letter to the post office when you're done, if you want. It closes at noon on Saturdays." He stands there, rubbing his mouth, then says, "You, uh, you mind if I read it?"

Read Mom's letter! But she wrote it to *me*.

Though I don't like it, I say, "Guess not."

FJ shakes his head slightly as he reads the letter. "You ever meet this Ricky?" he asks, frowning.

"No sir."

After he returns to letter to me, he picks up my pencil and jots down "Web County Texas Jail" on a page in my notebook. I watch as he tears out the page and folds it into his pocket.

"Okay, then," he says.

As FJ turns to leave, he notices the Chore List taped to the wall. "Oh, I've been meaning to tell you. Now that fall is here, you can cross off 'cut the grass' and add 'sweep and rake leaves.' And soon as leaves are done, you'll take your turn shoveling snow."

"Snow!"

He pauses. "You ever seen snow, Frankie Joe?"

"No sir, but I always wanted to. When's it gonna snow?"

"Hard to predict, but most likely around December." He looks thoughtful. "You bring a coat? A warm one?"

"Never needed one."

"I'll have Lizzie pick one up for you. And some warm clothes, too. She can get a discount." As he heads down the stairs, he says, "Better get to that homework now."

I groan. Chores and homework. Is that all he knows?

10:12 A.M.

Dear Mom,

Things are OK. The food is soso here, too. Except I got four stupid half brothers!!! I got a room of my own but I have to study a lot and do chores.

Let me know what that lawyer says, OK? You think maybe you'll be out by Xmas? I can hardly wait to see you, too.

Love ya loads,
Frankie Joe
XOXOXO

I want Mom to write again soon, but I know she won't. She hates writing letters. It's just the way she is, which is probably why Miss Peachcott never heard from her after she left Clearview. "Anything I got to say will be old news by the time the letter arrives," she used to say. "Besides, I got better things to do with my time."

I put my letter into an envelope and put a stamp on it, then slip it into my backpack so I can take it to the post office on the way to school on Monday. I'm afraid if I give it to FJ to mail, he might read it.

I look for a safe place to keep Mom's letter—safe from prying eyes. Spying the memento that Mrs. Jones gave me, I slide the letter inside the back, under the dust cover. I put the book back on the shelf, between my rock-collecting guide and the paint sample from Mr. Lopez.

The perfect place. My mementos from home are all together.

Sunday, October 4

8:00 A.M.

Hot water steams me from head to toe. FJ came up to the second floor this morning to enforce the new rule Lizzie made yesterday about showers. Matt was sullen as a bulldog when I got first dibs on the bathroom.

"But Dad," he protested. "I've always been first."

"Fair's fair," FJ told him. "I expect the new rule to be followed—to the letter."

FJ walked back downstairs as I walked inside the bathroom.

"...seventy-five, seventy-six...." I'm counting to a hundred–twenty to make sure I don't go over my two-minute limit—

What's that? I take my head from underneath the nozzle to listen, but decide I was hearing hot water gurgling in the pipes.

I hurry rinsing off, so I don't run over my time. As I slide the shower curtain open, I see my shorts—tied in a knot and floating in the toilet.

Great! It wasn't water in the pipes.

I wring my shorts out as best I can, but Matt's not cutting me any slack. Listening to him pound on the door for his turn, I pull on wet shorts and my jeans. Within seconds my crotch isn't just damp, it's soggy.

Leaving the bathroom, I find the ninja posse lined up in the hallway. Matt has a cocky grin on his face. The other three smother giggles.

I know Matt's the one who did it—his way of getting even. The others are just following along.

"Look," Matt says as I walk past. "The jailbird's kid wet his pants." He points to my wet crotch. "Now we've got *two* with bladder-control problems living here." He's still laughing when he goes into the bathroom.

Two? I see tears stream down Mark's face.

"You told," Mark blubbers through the bathroom door. "You said you wouldn't tell!"

I continue down the hall and up the stairs to the attic. Pulling off my wet jeans and shorts, I hang them over the back of the desk chair and put on dry clothes.

I can hear the brothers on the floor below. As one finishes showering and it's time for the next one, the showers get shorter and shorter—a sign the hot water is running out. I figure that Matt took longer than his two minutes. I feel sorry for Little Johnny, who is back to being last today.

It's only once every five days, I think. That's better than every day.

Creak. A hear another noise as I'm slipping my feet into socks. Mark's head appears above the landing, then the rest of his body snakes up the stairs.

"What do you want?" I snap.

His head hangs low. "I don't do it all the time, you know. I mean, I only have an accident when I'm too tired to wake up."

I had an accident once, I remember. I was at Felipe's Market one Saturday, and a man with a gun came in. He made all of us lie down on the floor while he cleaned out the till. I had to stand in front of everyone later— the customers, the police who came to investigate, *everyone*—in wet jeans that smelled like pee.

"Accidents happen," I say, shrugging. "Once when I was a little kid, I got so scared I peed myself."

"You did?" Mark's face relaxes, then immediately screws up again. "You, uh, you won't tell anyone, will you? I mean, I'm not as old as the rest of the kids in my class 'cause I skipped a grade."

Yeah, I know. You've got an "excellent brain."

"They'll make my life miserable if you tell," he goes on.

"I won't tell." I pull on my shoes and tie the laces.

"Promise?" Mark's eyes have a pleading look in them.

"Sure. Guess it's not easy being the smartest kid in school...or the dumbest."

"It's not." He hesitates. "You want, I can help you

with your schoolwork. Mom's helping you with spelling, maybe I can help you with math. That's my best subject."

I don't like a fourth-grader—especially one who should be a third-grader—reminding me that I'm slow.

"Thanks, but I'm doing okay." When Mark still doesn't leave, I give him a look. "What?"

"Nothin'. I just thought I'd walk with you to breakfast. I smelled ham, which means Mom will have applesauce with it. I *love* ham and applesauce."

"Yeah? Well, let's go." I've never had applesauce with ham, but it sounds good. On the way downstairs, my nose fills with goods smells that make my stomach growl.

"Race you to the kitchen," Mark says. When he reaches the bottom floor, he takes off running.

Before I can think, my legs start pumping for all they're worth. I catch him midway down the hall and burst through the kitchen door a length ahead of him.

"You won!" Mark yells. "I had a head start, and you beat me! *Kowabunga, dude*! You are freaky fast!"

Freaky *fast*. I like it.

FJ and Lizzie and the other boys are sitting at the table, looking at us like an explanation is in order.

"Well," I say, shrugging. "Some get excellent brains and some get long legs."

Everyone laughs. Except Matt.

5:10 P.M.

Lizzie stops me at the foot of the stairs as I'm going up to start homework. She and FJ are going to a meeting.

"Did I mention that I spoke with Mrs. Bixby today? She's planning to start tutoring you next Saturday at Quilt Circle. Isn't that great?"

"Um..." I let it go at that.

"We'll just be gone an hour or so," she continues. "These Oktoberfest planning meetings don't last long. I'm in charge of the Quilt Booth. That's when we start selling chances on our Christmas quilt."

"Octo—*What*?"

"*Oktoberfest*. It's an annual festival that's held here. There's a parade and booths, even live entertainment. Everyone comes. It's a lot of fun." She turns to FJ. "Okay, I'm ready."

He points to a check lying on the hall table. "Did you intend to leave that there?"

What? It's not safe to leave a check around with a jailbird's kid in the house?

"Yes, I did. Thanks for reminding me." Lizzie calls Matt to the front door. "Miss Peachcott's making deliveries today and plans to drop off my Nova order." She looks between Matt and me. "When she comes, one of you give her this check. Okay?"

"Oh," I say, feeling dumb. "Well, I was going upstairs to do homework, but sure—"

"I'll take care of it," Matt says, taking over. "You know you can depend on me."

Mr. Responsibility!

After FJ and Lizzie leave, Huckaby Number Two gives me a flinty look. First I pushed him out of slot Number One. Then I ruined his long, hot shower routine. Now I've been given equal responsibility with him. Not wanting to get into it with him, I double-time it up the stairs.

I'm sitting at the desk doing long division when I hear the front door slam. Through the window, I see Matt ride his bike into the street. Before I know it, the entire block fills up with Matt's friends.

Mandy's out there, too. She sees me through the window and waves me to come down, but I wave her off. She's insistent, so I open the window.

"I got homework," I call to her.

Matt slows down when he hears me. He circles in front of my window and yells to the others. "Hey, did you know Frankie Joe got a letter yesterday from his jailbird mama? She got arrested for dealing dope!"

Things screech to a stop. I see Mandy's mouth drop open. Everyone's mouth drops open.

"Jailbird's kid...jailbird's kid," Matt yells again and again. A few of the other kids take up the chant, too.

Mandy starts yelling, "Shut up! Shut up!" at them.

I want to kill Matt.

As I pull back from the window, I see someone with a cane standing at the corner, watching.

Oh no...

Matt and his gang see Miss Peachcott, too, and take off down the street.

The doorbell rings.

Where are you, Mr. Responsibility?

I hear another ring.

I clump down the stairs and open the door. Miss Peachcott steps into the house and hands me a pink paper bag with NOVA printed on it. Silently she takes the check that I fumble into her hand.

"Um, thanks," I say, looking at the floor. Reaching out, she lifts my chin so that I have to look at her.

"You done something you're ashamed of, Frankie Joe Huckaby?"

"No ma'am. Not that I know of."

"Then you look people in this one-horse town in the eye. You understand?"

"Yes ma'am," I say, even though I don't.

She shuffles to the door and closes it behind her. As the door clicks shut, I understand what Miss Peachcott was telling me. Word about Mom being in jail will be all over town by tomorrow.

I want to cry. I leave the Nova bag on the hall table and climb the stairs, two at a time. At the desk, I push my notebook aside. I don't care if I flunk Math and English and History and Science. Fail *everything*. All I want to do is leave Clearview in my dust. I lay my head on the desk and squeeze my eyes shut.

Please please, I think, let Mom get out of jail early.

All at once, I have a startling thought. What if she does?

Raising my head, the first thing I see is the definition I wrote for *home* and the constant answer: The Lone Star Trailer Park.

"I'm going home," I whisper.

9:55 P.M.

By bedtime I've put together a runaway plan—my own "great escape." I've even found an empty cardboard box in the storage area to keep things I'll need for the trip. No one will notice it because it fits right in with the others.

I have to leave soon, I think, remembering that FJ said it would start snowing in December. That means I'll get home before Mom does, but that's okay. I'll be there waiting for her, no matter when she gets out.

I review the list, thinking through every step to make sure I haven't overlooked anything.

Bedroll Maybe I can find one in an alley before the garbage men come.
Tarp It might rain. I'll look for one while I'm looking for a bedroll.
Spare bike tube and flat kit How am I gonna buy this? I don't have any money.

93

Pot for cooking There's always old pots and pans in alleys.

Matches to start a fire, and a Ziploc bag to keep them dry In the kitchen maybe.

Canteen Plenty of rivers along the way. I can recycle an empty plastic bottle.

Jacket FJ is taking care of that.

Bungee cord For strapping down stuff in my bike basket. I'll check the storage shed.

Money To buy food and other stuff I can't find for free.

Where am I gonna get money? Maybe the grocery store manager will let me sweep out the back room like I did at Felipe's Market.

"No way FJ will let me get a job," I mumble. "A job would interfere with my chores and homework."

What am I going to do?

Saturday, October 10

1:20 P.M.

Shush...shush...

Leaves are starting to fall fast. It's my chore to sweep them off the porch. Lizzie wants it clean when her quilt group arrives; but as soon as I get the leaves off, they're back again.

We all have regular chores to do and take turns doing other things. Clearing the table after meals, stacking the dishwasher, taking out the trash, yard work. The others got their chores done this morning because they have things to do Saturday afternoons—fun things. Matt rides along with FJ to visit farms. Mark goes to 4-H. Luke, to Chess Club. Little Johnny has karate. While he was waiting for his ride to pick him up, he ran around the house in his white trousers and jacket and belt, yelling, "kowabunga!"

I have leaves that won't stop falling—and Mrs. Bixby.

I watch a leaf devil race down the street, swirling into the sky like a miniature tornado. Back home in Texas, we have dirt devils, not leaf devils. I miss dirt. And rocks. I bet Mr. O'Hare's out looking for space rocks today...without me.

The front door squeaks as it opens. "Want a cookie?" Lizzie steps onto the porch. "Fresh out of the oven."

"Um, sure." I set my broom aside and take an oatmeal-and-raisin cookie. I wish Lizzie wasn't so nice to me. I want to hate her as much as I hate everything else in Clearview. Liking her makes me feel like I'm being a traitor to Mom.

Clunk...thump.

I recognize the noises coming from the front room. FJ is setting up Lizzie's quilting frame. The Quilt Circle will be meeting soon, which means Mrs. Bixby will be here, too. I can't believe my luck. To have to face fidgety-eyed Mrs. Bixby five days a week *and* on Saturday afternoons. Last week she had me read in front of the whole group. It was humiliating.

It's just not fair. The Huckaby brothers go their happy-go-lucky ways on Saturday afternoons. Not me.

"Take another cookie," Lizzie says. "I made plenty."

"Thanks." As I chew, I wonder what I'll be made to do today. Read? Say my multiplication tables? Recite important dates in history?

As Lizzie goes back inside the house to finish setting

up, I sit down on the front steps to watch Matt. Until FJ is ready to leave, Huckaby Number Two is racing his bike with some other kids. They stir up the leaves in the gutters, making them swirl overhead.

The Huckaby house has been designated the official finish line, so I have a front row seat. Matt comes in first every time. The racing tires on his bike help a lot, but he knows how to run a race, too.

I watch as he starts out, pumping hard and fast. Shifting into a faster gear once he's going good. And leaning forward at the finish line so his weight carries him forward. No two ways about it, Matt's fast.

Wonder if I could beat him....

"Hey, Oddball. When are you gonna stop hidin' out?" Mandy rides up next to the front steps on her old Mongoose BMX with twenty-inch wheels. It's almost as beat up as my Rover Sport. She's been bugging me for two weeks to participate, ever since Matt opened his mouth about Mom being in jail.

"I'm not hidin' out."

She drops her bike to the ground and sits down next to me. "Um, I got an uncle who went to jail." She glances at me sideways. "He drank too much and got thrown in the drunk tank—"

"Shut up, Mandy."

"Okay."

She manages to stay quiet a couple of seconds.

"Did I tell you Miss Peachcott ordered more cookies? I took by her order, and she bought a bunch more. Isn't that great?"

"Yeah, *great.*"

"You don't mean that," she says, looking hurt.

I feel bad. Mandy is okay.

"No joke," I say, looking at her, "that's really great."

"Miss Peachcott asked about you. She'd like it if you came to see her. She said her project wasn't going so good—whatever that means."

I decide Miss Peachcott is okay, too.

"Well, you should go see her sometime," Mandy says when I don't say anything.

"Yeah, whatever."

"Oh, stop pouting," she says, poking me in the rib with her elbow. "C'mon, grab your bike. Bet I can beat you."

"In your dreams—"

The front door squeaks again, and FJ walks outside.

"Hi, Mr. Huckaby."

"Hey, Mandy. How are you?"

"Okay. Trying to talk Frankie Joe into biking with me. He's being pigheaded."

FJ looks at me. "Why won't you go? Lot of fun, riding your bike through leaves. I did it when I was a kid."

"Not in the mood," I say. "Besides, I got chores to do and"—I nod toward the living room—"it's...you know, Saturday."

Mandy climbs back on her bike. "That's not the *real* reason he won't ride." Giving me a *so-there!* look, she wheels across the yard and bumps over the curb into the street.

I want to strangle her.

FJ sits down next to me. "Look, Frankie Joe. If I could, I'd buy you another bike, but it's not in the budget right now. I'm real sorry you're stuck with a trash bike, but—"

"It's not a trash bike," I say, feeling angry. "Mr. O'Hare was a mechanic in the air force. He worked on jet planes! He helped me fix it. It's as good as any of those bikes *out there*." I jab my finger toward the street.

"Then what's Mandy talking about? What's the real reason you won't ride with them?"

Caught off guard, I blurt out the truth. " 'Cause they don't like me."

"What makes you think that?"

"The names they call me."

He looks at me like I'm corn or soybeans that he's analyzing. "What names?"

"Well, the one I hate most is Freaky Slow Frankie Joe." I know I've gone too far to turn back, so I keep talking. "They think I'm stupid because ... well, because I *am* stupid. Mark can do ratios, and I can't even count by sevens. Even Luke can count by sevens!"

FJ's mouth goes straight as a plank. "Don't ever let anyone tell you that. You are *not* stupid. You just didn't go to school like you should have and got behind. Your mother always was irresponsible...."

As FJ's voice trails off, he turns to face me. "Martha Jane made rash decisions, didn't think about the consequences. But that doesn't mean you're stupid. You hear me?"

"Yes sir." Part of me doesn't like what he says about Mom, but another part of me knows it's true. Her ending up in jail is proof of that.

"Good. Next time anyone says that to you, you tell them you just didn't go to school like you should and got behind. All right?"

"Yes sir," I mumble.

"Well, all right then."

We watch the boys riding bikes a while longer.

All at once, FJ says, "How about you ride out with me today? You've been working hard and could use a break. Matt can stay home and do the leaves. Since you've started sharing chores, the rest don't have as many to do."

For one heartbeat, I wonder what Matt will think about having to give Freaky Slow Frankie Joe a turn. I'm sure he'll find a way to make me pay.

Still I say, "Yes sir, I'd like to go. But, what about Mrs. Bixby?"

"I'll talk to Lizzie, then tell Matt."

I watch as FJ goes inside the house. When he returns,

he waves Matt to the curb. The two talk for a good bit. While I can't make out all their words, I'm certain more than just taking a turn is being discussed. One thing for certain, whatever else they're talking about is not making Matt happy. Even from the stoop, I can see his face turning red. But when I get the wave from FJ, I'm off the porch in a flash.

FJ climbs into the driver's seat of his work truck as I head for the passenger side. I have to go by red-faced Matt on the way.

"Kowabunga, dude," I whisper in passing.

1:45 P.M.

I stick my head out the window, looking at field after field of corn and soybeans. The sky is clear and bright blue, and the air, cool and fresh. The wind blows my hair back from my face, and the air fills my lungs so fast, I have to gulp to take it all in.

Freedom feels great! I want the day to never end.

"We're going to see a farmer named Puffin," FJ says. "*Mr.* Puffin."

I get it. Treat *Mr.* Puffin with respect because he grows corn and soybeans. And they pay the bills.

Roads running north and south intersect with others running east and west, straight as rulers. I feel like we're running a maze as FJ turns down first one road, then another. On every road, I see the same sign posted at the end of rows. The sign has a picture of an ear of corn on it—the corn painted bright yellow; the leaves, bright green—and the word *AgriGold*.

"What's that mean? AgriGold?"

FJ glances at the sign. "That's a type of corn farmers around here plant. Good tolerance to disease, heavy producer. It's called that because it's a big moneymaker. You know, *agri*–culture and gold. Gold's another way of saying money."

"Oh, I get it."

He glances at me. "Grow more grain crops here than any other country. That's why it's called the Bread Basket of the World."

Yeah, I learned that in kindergarten.

I regret telling FJ that I'm stupid. Now *he's* treating me like I'm slow.

We drive close enough to look inside the red barns I saw on the way up from Texas. FJ points out tractors and spreaders, pickers and harvesters stored inside. We get close enough to the missile-size blue silos to read the word *Harvestore* on their sides.

Cool. Harvest + Store = Harvestore.

FJ looks at me, and I figure he's getting ready to explain it to me.

"I get it," I blurt before he can speak. "Harvest plus Store equals Harvestore. I'm not *that* dumb."

FJ gives his head a little shake. "I know, Frankie

Joe. We just talked about that. That's not what I was going to say."

"It wasn't?"

"No." He turns down a lane leading to a big white house. "Mr. Puffin's wife died last year, so be sensitive with what you say. He's still grieving."

Now I do feel dumb.

An old man is waiting for us. He wears a sweaty ball cap, plaid flannel shirt, faded blue dungarees, and leather work boots. Behind him I see black-and-white cows behind a long row of bushes.

I pinch my nose as we get out of the truck. "Wow, what's that *stink*?"

FJ shakes his head.

What'd I do?

The old man laughs and points to piles of manure in the pasture. "You get used to it after a while. Except Mary never did. That's why she planted all them lilac bushes." He waves an arm toward the row of shrubs next to the pasture. "Lilacs hide the smell of manure. Too bad they don't bloom year round."

FJ shakes hands with Mr. Puffin and introduces me. "Frankie Joe's my oldest boy..."

Yeah, I think. The dumb, insensitive one.

"...and he's staying with us for a spell."

I can see the curiosity in the old man's eyes, but he just holds his hand out to me so I can shake it.

"Pleased to meet you," I say. "Sorry to hear of your loss." I give FJ a how-was-that? look.

He gives me a smile, then looks toward the pasture. "When are you gonna give up these cows, Harvey? I doubt they're making you enough to pay for their keep."

"Probably right, Frank. But I got nothin' better to do, now Mary's gone."

I trail behind FJ and Mr. Puffin as they pull ears of corn off stalks, peel back husks, and talk about how the ears are filling out. Watching them puncture kernels with their thumbnails to test for moisture, I ask if I can try.

"Sure thing." Mr. Puffin pulls another ear off a stalk and hands it to me. "You know why too much moisture's bad?"

"Frankie Joe's not from around here," FJ says quickly, "so he doesn't know about such things…"

I feel my shoulders droop. I'm back to being dumb.

"…but I'm sure he'd like to learn."

Mr. Puffin turns to me. "You don't want too much moisture 'cause then the corn has to dry before we can store it. You don't, it'll mold."

"I know what mold is." I think about of our refrigerator back in Texas. "Mold grows on food, and you have to throw it out. Except on cheese; you can cut it off of cheese."

"That's right," Mr. Puffin says. "What about shrink on corn? You know what that is?"

"No sir."

"It's the weight loss that occurs during the drying process. It's better if the corn dries natural in the field, else we have to use mechanical processes to dry it out. That's costly, affects your profit."

I push my thumbnail into a kernel to see how dry it is.

"Smell it," he tells me.

"The corn?"

"Yeah. See if it smells musty or sour or garlicky."

Garlicky? I take a sniff as he tells me about other things that can affect profit, like smut balls and insect infestation.

"Smut's a fungus that looks just like what it's called—black soot—but it's really a parasite." He grins. "And I'm sure you know what bugs like to eat."

"Corn and beans," I say, grinning, too.

After the corn, we move to another field and do similar kinds of tests on soybeans. I learn how to pop open the shells and run my thumb inside the pale green pods to break the beans loose. I also learn about orange ladybugs that eat tiny insects called "aphids," which suck the sap out of plants. We walk up and down rows of soybeans, eyeballing the leaves and plants for signs of fungus and insect damage, which can stunt the plant and affect yield.

"Good shrink on the corn, Harvey," FJ says at the end of all the eyeballing and squeezing and smelling. "Beans look good, too."

The old man looks pleased when FJ makes his final assessment. We walk back toward the house through corn so tall the sky all but disappears. The long leaves on the corn wrap around me, making me feel invisible.

A person could disappear in all this corn....

Before I know it, I'm thinking about my plan to light out for Texas. Seeing my friends again. Telling Mr. O'Hare about the farm machinery inside the big barns. Describing the color of the ladybugs to Mr. Lopez. Talking to Mrs. Jones about blight and aphids on corn and soybeans. Being free to ride my bike any time I want. To smell mesquite. Taste the sand that blows in off the Chihuahua Desert. Spook up birds and deer, hunt space rocks—and be there to welcome Mom when she gets home.

I can just ride straight south on those ruler-straight roads and eat my way back home, I decide. As tall as the corn grows, I could even hide out in it to escape the real posse I'm sure FJ would send after me.

I'll need to be careful, not slip up....

"These fields look like they run on forever," I say, figuring this is a good chance to test out my escape route. "I bet they run all the way down the middle of the country."

Mr. Puffin doesn't skip a beat. "Well sir, that's a fact."

That's the best thing I've learned all afternoon.

3:15 P.M.

"All your hard work's paid off, Harvey," FJ says. "If it doesn't rain, you'll end up with a top-grade crop this year."

"Well then, let us pray it doesn't rain. Don't need any hiccups now that would set the harvest back." Mr. Puffin looks at FJ and asks, "Got time for a cup?"

"Been waiting all day for a cup of your good coffee, Harvey."

The sun has begun to lower in the west when I follow Mr. Puffin into the white-painted farmhouse. I don't like that the day is almost over.

As I sit down at the kitchen table, Mr. Puffin asks, "What's got you so long in the jaw, boy?" He sets about making a fresh pot of coffee. "You hungry? I bet you're hungry."

"Um, no sir." It's because I have to go back to the Huckaby house, but I can't tell him that because FJ is sitting across from me.

FJ gives me a look, and I remember that I'm supposed to be sensitive. "Well, maybe a *little* hungry," I say to Mr. Puffin.

"Well, I'd be a *lot* hungry, I was a growing boy like you. What's your favorite thing to eat?" He searches through cupboards and the refrigerator.

"Burritos," I say.

"Burritos!" Mr. Puffin pulls a package of

store-bought cookies from a bread box on the counter. "That's Mexican food, isn't it? I like Italian food myself. Pepperoni-and-sausage pizza's my favorite. That place in Clearview makes the best pepperoni-and-sausage pizza I ever ate. You like pizza?"

"Sure do."

Mr. Puffin shakes some rock-hard cookies onto a plate and sets it on the table. "Me too. Haven't had a slice in better'n a year now."

"Why, Harvey," FJ says, "you're not but...what, seven miles from town? Why don't you just drive in and pick one up?"

"Seven miles?" I say. "That's nothin'! I bet I do seventy miles a day when I bike in the Chihuahua Desert. I can do seven miles in fifteen minutes—no, ten!"

FJ looks skeptical.

"That might be," Mr. Puffin says, "but I milk cows mornin' and night, seven days a week. Have to clean the milk shed when I'm done, too." The old man's eyes begin to look wet. "Used to be, Mary cleaned the milking shed, and we'd get done early enough to run into town." He pours two cups of coffee and sets them on the table. "But no more."

"One of those big dairies would buy those cows off you, Harvey," FJ says. "Why don't you give it some thought?"

"Long as I've known you, Frank, you've been right

more than you been wrong. I'll think on it." Mr. Puffin pours a glass of milk and sets it in front of me.

My mind takes off on its own as I dunk hockey-puck cookies into milk. "I could bring you a pizza," I blurt out.

"What?" FJ's eyes open wide.

"I'd do my homework before I leave. I mean, it's *only* seven miles out and seven miles back."

Mr. Puffin laughs. "Sounds like the boy needs a break from all that studying." He shakes his head, looking unsure. "You'd have to figure out a way to carry it."

"I already got a basket on my bike for carrying things. I delivered things for people in Laredo."

"That a fact? How much did you charge?"

"Tips. I worked for tips."

Mr. Puffin shakes his head. "Delivery charge would be better. So much a mile, maybe." Turning to FJ, he says, "I'm open for it. What do you think?"

A rare thing happens: FJ smiles.

"How far out and back would that be, Frankie Joe?" he asks. "You know, seven times two?"

"Huh? Oh, seven times two is...fourteen. Fourteen miles is easy."

"And if you come out twice a month, how many miles would it be? Round trip. In other words, four trips at seven miles each."

Is he serious? Two times a month away from the mutant ninja posse *and* the Saturday Quilt Circle?

My heart begins to pound. "Uh, that would be... twenty-eight miles."

Oh—he's teaching me to count by sevens!

"And what if you come out *four* times a month?"

My heart flip-flops like a Mexican jumping bean. I never dreamed I'd have a reason to count by sevens, but now I do: to earn money to get back home.

I'm so excited I can't think straight. "I don't know right now, but I'll figure it out before we leave today!"

"Okay then," says FJ. "You can do it if..."

I hold my breath.

"...you wear a helmet. Won't have you out on the road without one. I'm sure we have a spare one at the house."

"I never wear a helmet." I watch FJ's smile turn to a frown. "But okay. I'll wear a helmet." I'll do anything to get free of Mrs. Bixby and the Quilt Circle on Saturdays.

"Well now," Mr. Puffin says, raising his eyebrows at FJ. "You've got an enterprising boy here."

Enterprising? I wonder if that's a good thing.

Mr. Puffin asks, "You got a name for your new business?"

"Yes sir," I say without hesitating. "Frankie Joe's Freaky Fast Delivery Service."

en·ter·pris·ing \ *adj* **:** marked by an indepen-
dent energetic spirit and by readiness to under-
take or experiment.

I read the definition again before I close the dictionary, thinking, Mandy's not the only one who's good at
business.

Impatient to get started, I decide to make a sign for
my bike. I search out a scrap piece of cardboard in the
storage part of the attic and find a felt-tip marker in the
desk drawer. In my best penmanship, I letter FRANKIE
JOE'S FREAKY FAST DELIVERY SERVICE.

Creeping downstairs I go to the kitchen where I
know Lizzie keeps twist-ties from bread wrappers. I
find four, then look for an ice pick in her odds-and-ends
drawer. I punch holes in the four corners of the cardboard and push the plastic twist ties through. With
everything I need to secure the sign to my bike basket,
I head for the front porch. In a matter of minutes, the
sign is wired on my basket, and I'm in business.

I sneak back upstairs to my bedroom and turn in.
Lying in bed, I stare at the ceiling and think about my
escape-to-Texas plan. I decide to add maps to my list,
just to be on the safe side.

FJ can get more free from Triple A if he needs
them... but I bet he won't be driving back to Texas

again. As soon as I'm back with Mom, things will go back to normal.

As I drift off to sleep, I start to dream. It's the day I arrived in Clearview, Illinois. I'm sitting at the table with all the Huckabys, and Lizzie asks me to tell everyone what I'm good at. I hear myself say, "Enterprising. I'm enterprising."

Friday, October 16

4:50 P.M.

"How much you gonna charge for delivery?"

It's Friday afternoon, and Mandy's invited herself to walk home with me. She's excited that I'm going to be delivering pizzas on Saturdays, starting tomorrow.

"Depends on how far it is," I tell her.

We scuff our feet through leaves, which are really dropping now that October is half gone. The leaves aren't pukey green anymore. Now they're the color of dirty gym socks.

"I figure a quarter a mile is fair," I say. "That would be a dollar seventy-five for seven miles—that's how far it is to Mr. Puffin's place."

"Sounds a little cheap to me. It's a round-trip, you know."

"Yeah, I know, but I wanna be fair." I don't tell her that my new business has an extra benefit. It gets me away from the Kowabunga gang and Mrs. Bixby.

"How do you plan on keeping the pizzas hot?"

"Uh-oh. Didn't think of that."

"I bet Mr. Gambino would help figure something out. Since he runs the pizza parlor, selling more pizzas would help him out, too."

"Yeah, that makes sense."

"Come on, let's go talk to him."

A few minutes later, we're inside the pizza place, where Mandy points out Mr. Gambino. He's talking to a man standing at the counter who's paying his check.

"This is Frankie Joe," Mandy tells Mr. Gambino when he finishes with his customer. "He's starting a pizza-delivery business."

"A pizza-delivery business! Well that's good."

"Hey, I heard about you," the man who just paid says.

"This is Mr. Lindholm," Mr. Gambino tells me.

"You're that enterprisin' boy my neighbor Harvey Puffin mentioned," Mr. Lindholm says. "My place is right next to his." He pauses. "Say, how about you bring one along for me, too? Gonna be gettin' real busy."

I'm speechless. *Two* customers?

Mandy pokes me in the ribs. "Um, yes sir, I could do that," I say. "Only I don't have an insulated bag to keep the pizzas hot."

I turn to Mr. Gambino. "That's what I came to ask you about."

"Insulated bag..." Mr. Gambino disappears into the backroom for several minutes. "I knew I kept this thing for a reason," he says when he returns. He hands me a dust-coated plastic bag with a zipper. "It holds two, maybe three pizza boxes."

I can't believe my luck. "Thanks! Thanks a lot!"

"Not doin' me any good stuck in the storeroom. It's left over from old times when Clearview was busier." He sighs. "Them days is gone. Now I have to run a twofer on Friday nights to get people to come in."

"Not anymore," Mandy says, grinning at me.

Before Mandy and I leave, I arrange to pick up two pizzas the next afternoon: a pepperoni and sausage for Mr. Puffin and a meat-lover's for Mr. Lindholm.

"You'll have to trust me until I get paid," I tell Mr. Gambino. "Soon as I get back to town, I'll bring you your money." I hold my breath, knowing he's probably heard that my mother is in jail.

"I got no problem with that," he says.

"Thanks," I say to Mandy when we're outside.

"We businesspeople have to stick together," she says. "Anyway, I owed you one. Miss Peachcott turned out to be a good customer." She pauses. "You been by to see her yet?"

"I've been busy."

She raises her eyebrows at me.

"Really," I say. "You don't have the homework I do."

Or a mother in jail that Miss Peachcott is bound to ask about.

"*Sure,*" she says. Her eyebrows go up again.

I'm going to have to get better at this lying business.

Saturday, October 17

3:15 P.M.

The cardboard sign on the front of my bike flaps like a bird because I'm pedaling so fast. I have two pizzas in the insulated bag on my bike basket, one for Mr. Puffin and one for his neighbor, Mr. Lindholm. Because the bag is so big, I used a bungee cord to strap it on top of the basket to keep the pizzas from sliding around inside. It was Lizzie's idea. She found the bungee on her back porch.

I can use it on my escape, too.

I memorized the map FJ drew showing me all the roads and turns to get to Mr. Puffin's and Mr. Lindholm's. But I still pause at corners to read county road markers, just to make sure I don't get turned around. The corn is so tall, it's hard to tell which direction I'm going.

I begin to worry about getting lost on my trip home. Then I remember something Mr. O'Hare taught me once when we were hunting rocks in the desert.

"Let the sun be your guide, Frankie Joe. Just remember that it rises in the east and sets in the west. And when it's warmin' the top of your head, it's high noon."

I'm relieved to see LINDHOLM on a mailbox next to the road. As I turn into the drive, I see a man walking to a big red barn. "It's me, Mr. Lindholm," I call out. "With one extra-large meat-lover's to go."

"Just in time, Frankie Joe." He laughs. "My stomach's turning inside out." He pulls a billfold out of his overalls.

I remove the pizza box marked MEAT-LOVER'S and hand it to him. Mr. Gambino has taped the cash-register receipt to the top of the box that shows the price. "Eleven ninety-eight, with tax," I read off. "And a dollar seventy-five delivery charge."

He hands me two bills: a ten and a five.

Oh no! I forgot about making change.

"I'll have to owe you the difference." I show him my empty pockets.

"Keep the rest," Mr. Lindholm says. "With the cost of gas these days, you're a bargain. Now I got to get this inside quick. My wife is waitin'. I bet Harvey's waitin' on his, too."

"Yes sir. I'm on my way."

"I'll give him a call, let him know you're comin'."

Mr. Lindholm waves, and I start pedaling. It's only

another half mile to Mr. Puffin's house, a few minutes at most. I'm flying when I race down his lane.

"Hi, Mr. Puffin." I screech to a stop at his kitchen door.

He's waiting for me, money in his hand. "Max called, told me you was coming."

I remove the pizza box from the insulated container and say, "Still hot." I take the two bills he hands me. Another ten and a five. "Um, I forgot to bring change, but—"

He waves me off. "Keep the rest for a tip."

Wow! Three-fifty for delivery, and another two-fifty in tips. Six dollars! I'll have enough money to go home before you know it.

"You wanna come in for a slice, Frankie Joe? This is a mighty big pizza for one person, and I bet you worked up an appetite on the way out."

Did I ever! My stomach growled all the way. I want a slice of pizza really bad, but I'm afraid that FJ will be mad if I'm late getting back...or that Lizzie might worry.

Fat chance. They have four "weeds" to think about.

I remember then that Mr. Puffin doesn't have a wife waiting inside, and the words come easy. "I was hopin' you'd say that, Mr. Puffin. A slice of pizza would be great."

4:55 P.M.

"Wouldn't have taken but a minute to let us know you were running late," FJ says.

I'm standing in the living room when he dresses me down. In front of Huckaby Numbers Two, Three, Four, and Five, who are sitting on the sofa grinning like monkeys.

"You're the one told me to be sensitive 'cause he's grieving."

"I don't mind you stayed to visit with Harvey," he snaps, "but he has a phone." He glances at Lizzie, who is standing beside him. "You worried your mother."

She's not my mother!

"It was very thoughtful of you to do that," Lizzie says as she pulls on a sweater. She and FJ are getting ready to leave for a meeting. "Just give us a call next time, okay?"

"Yes ma'am," I say, staring at the floor.

She smiles, then looks at me and the other boys. "Oh, I signed you all up to ride in the Oktoberfest parade. It's on the thirty-first, so you need to get streamers on your bikes before then."

Streamers? No way!

"Okay," the four "weeds" say in unison.

"There's a good movie on The Disney Channel tonight," Lizzie says, "and I made a batch of cereal-snack mix. I put two liters of soda in the frig, too, but only use one. I don't care which, but save the other one for tomorrow. Understood?"

I nod, and the half brothers sing out, "Understood."

As soon as they're gone, Johnny plops onto the footstool in front of the TV. Mark and Luke sprawl on the oval rug on either side of him. Matt scrunches up on one end of the sofa, and I scrunch up on the other—a no-man's land in between.

"Hey, let's fix our drinks now," Luke says just before the movie starts. "That way we won't miss any of it. The commercials are only a minute-and-a-half long. That's ninety seconds, not enough time for us to get our drinks."

"Jeez, Luke," Mark groans. "How do you know how long the commercials are?"

"I timed them."

Luke leads us to the kitchen and pulls five glasses from the cupboard. Mark removes a tray of ice from the freezer and pops cubes into the glasses. Matt opens the refrigerator door and takes out a liter of cola.

"Wait," Johnny says. "I want orange."

"Well, you're getting cola!" says Matt.

Johnny's bottom lip starts to quiver.

"Don't be a crybaby," Matt says. "You can have orange tomorrow."

"Um, I actually want orange, too," Mark says. "We had cola last time."

"Too...bad," Matt says, making his voice sound whiny.

"I wanna vote," Johnny pipes up.

"Vote?" Matt stares at him. "What do you mean, vote?"

Mark jumps in. "Yeah! Remember what Mom said about odd-numbered families? Let's take a vote."

Before I can protest, Numbers Three, Four, and Five yell, "Vote...vote...vote!"

Matt's eyes turn slitty. "You want a vote," he growls, "then we vote. I vote for cola." He looks at Luke. "What do you want, Luke? Mark and Johnny already decided."

No fair. He's putting Luke on the spot.

Vote for orange, I eye-telegraph Luke. But when Luke takes a step backward, I read the writing on the wall.

"I guess cola's okay with me," he says. "But, uh, that makes it a tie, so"—he turns to me—"that means you have to be the tiebreaker, Frankie Joe."

I want to strangle Luke. I don't want to be the tie-breaker. What do I care what flavor soda we have?

I shake my head and turn toward the door. "Leave me outta this."

"No fair," Johnny says. He's blocking the doorway like he's a three-hundred-pound tackle instead of a forty-pound first-grader. "You gotta play by the rules."

Great. Now Little Johnny's throwing rules at me. I suck the spit from between my front teeth. I have nine months to go until Mom gets out of jail, and if I buck Matt, he'll make my life miserable the whole time—

Wait! I'll be long gone before then!

"I vote for orange," I blurt out, looking at Matt.

"Orange it is!" Luke uncaps the bottle and sloshes orange soda into glasses. Everyone grabs a glass and heads back to the front room.

On the way, Luke sidles up to me. "Thanks," he whispers, "I really wanted orange, too. We have cola ninety-eight percent of the time 'cause it's Matt's favorite. It gets real boring."

Matt's the first one back to the living room, only he doesn't sit down on the sofa. He takes over the footstool in front of the television.

"You're too big," Johnny says. "Let me sit there."

"Yeah, move over," Mark says. "We can't see."

But Matt won't budge. Mark and Luke lay down on either side of him so they can catch a sliver of the screen. Little Johnny settles next to me on the sofa, where we see a little of the movie and a lot of Matt's head. For the first time in four weeks, I get the feeling that I'm not the only one who hates Matt's guts.

The movie's a science-fiction flick, one of my favorite kinds, but I want to search the attic for things on my escape to Texas plan. I don't like taking things that don't belong to me, but as soon as I get back to Texas and make some more money, I plan to pay for anything I take. I have the six dollars I made today hidden in my cardboard box in the storage area, but I need it for the trip home.

As soon as I finish my soda, I slide off the sofa.

"Where ya goin'?" Johnny asks.

"To my room to study," I whisper.

"But why? It's Saturday night. We don't gotta study on Saturday nights."

I wish for a roll of duct tape to use on his mouth. "Yeah, but I want my grades to get better."

Mark rolls over and looks at me. "You don't need to worry. I overheard two of the teachers at school talking about you."

I hesitate. "What'd they say?"

"That you're improving fast."

I'm improving?

"Yeah," Luke chimes in. "I saw Dad at school today. He met with Mr. Arnt, and I heard him say that you're doing good."

FJ's having school conferences with Mr. Arnt and didn't tell me?

"Well...that's great," I say, "but I still want to go upstairs to study."

Matt turns around slowly and looks at me. "Family rule is NO studying on Saturday night. Why are you insisting on going upstairs?" His eyes are back to slits.

Maybe I shouldn't have gotten so cocky.

"Yeah, well it's not a very good movie. I'd rather read a book." I leave the room, glancing over my shoulder at Matt. He's watching every step I take, his eyes like daggers.

I'm going to have to be very, very careful around him.

Wednesday, October 21

5:35 P.M.

"There's more groceries in the van," Lizzie says. Matt and I are setting the table for supper. "One of you want to bring them in?"

"I'll get them," I say. In the van, I search hurriedly for the Triple A maps and find them stuck in a side pocket. I don't feel too bad taking them because I know FJ can get maps free from Triple A. Stuffing them under my shirt, I carry the grocery bag inside and set it on the counter.

"Be back in a minute," I say to Lizzie. Hurrying upstairs, I hide the maps in the box with my money stash.

"Where'd you go?" Matt asks when I get back to the kitchen.

"Bathroom to wash up." Ever since I left the room early on movie night, Matt's been watching me like a hawk.

"Why didn't you use the one down here?"

"Didn't think about it." When his eyes become slits, I decide to take out the trash.

"Frankie Joe volunteered to bring in the groceries," Lizzie tells FJ when I get back. As we sit down to eat, she smiles approvingly at me. So does FJ.

I put a fake-mouth smile on my face, feeling like a traitor.

"Suck up," Matt whispers.

8:45 P.M.

I bury my head in the Triple A maps, calculating mileage between Clearview and Laredo. I'm glad now that FJ marked all the highways with a yellow highlighter because it means I don't have to do any navigating on my own. I'll take roads that run alongside them. County roads. Farm roads. Since I'll be able to hear the traffic on the highways, I won't lose my way.

A long column of numbers fills an entire notebook page—the mileage numbers between points on the maps for Illinois, Missouri, Oklahoma, and Texas. I add them up.

Fourteen hundred miles! Did we come that far?

Maybe we did. I slept a lot.

I look at my paper again to make sure I put the comma where it belonged. No mistakes.

One thousand, four hundred miles.

Wonder how long that's gonna take?

9:45 P.M.

An hour later, I'm still working—doing calculations and checking my answers and making adjustments for bumpy back roads and hiding out in cornfields. Finally I'm satisfied.

"Fifty miles a day. I can do that easy."

I divide total miles by my daily average: 1400 divided by 50 equals 28 days.

"A month! A month to make the trip that took us two days to drive!" My stomach starts to hurt. "Jeez, I can't do this....It's too long....I'll never make it."

Mr. O'Hare wouldn't give up. The voice comes from inside my head. *He's been looking for a space rock for ages and still goes out every day. He'd never give up.*

"Yeah...he wouldn't. And I'm not a quitter, either."

I think back to my going-away party at Mrs. Jones's. She told me to look upon my trip here as an adventure. And now the trip home will really be one.

I start to feel better. Even excited.

"Lights out, Frankie Joe," FJ calls from the bottom of the stairs.

"Yes sir," I say.

I fold up my work, put it into my backpack, and turn out the light. My plan is taking shape. All I have to do is make sure to leave before it snows.

All of a sudden, I feel disappointed. I really wanted to see snow.

Saturday, October 31

6:15 A.M.

It's still dark when I crawl out of bed and pull on my clothes. The stairs creak when I go downstairs, and I hope a certain someone doesn't hear me. Matt's been dogging my tracks ever since the night I made excuses for not watching the movie. I've had to get sneaky to find what I need for the trip. December and snow will be here in a month.

I slip out the back door and head for the storage shed, hoping to find an old tent or tarp. I've already found a ragged sleeping bag and a dented skillet in an alley, picked up before the garbagemen came. And I took a few Ziploc bags from the kitchen. I felt bad that I couldn't pay Lizzie for them. I plan to leave her a dollar when I go. I also plan to pay for the tarp or tent, too, if I find one in the shed.

If ninja-dog Matt will let me find one, that is. He's been on me like a bloodhound.

It's cold in the shed so I scrounge hurriedly through cardboard boxes stacked in the corner. I pull a blue polyurethane tarp out of one.

Pay dirt!

"What'cha doin' in there?" Matt stands in the doorway of the storage shed, his eyes drilling a hole in me.

"Looking," I say. "That a crime?"

"It is if you're planning on stealing whatever it is you're looking for."

Stealing? It's not really, I think, because I'm gonna pay for it when I leave. But I can't tell him that.

I decide to play dumb. "What makes you think I'm planning on stealing something?"

"Because you're being sneaky." He looks at the tarp I'm holding. "What're you planning on doing with that?"

Busted. No way out. I have to lie.

"Uh, I'm planning on setting my bike on it so I can grease the gears. They're sticking and, uh...the Oktoberfest parade's today. I got up early to fix them."

"If you weren't so stupid, Sneaky Freaky Slow Frankie Joe, you'd know grease would just gum up those gears. WD-40's what you need to use, and there's a can sitting right there on the workbench."

Yeah, I know. Mr. O'Hare taught me that. I'm just a bad liar.

"Oh, right," I say. I put the tarp back into the box and return it to the shelf.

Matt hesitates before going back in the house. "I know what's up, you know."

"You do?" My heart thumps. How did he figure out that I'm planning to run away?

"Yeah, and I'm gonna find a way to stop it. Then you won't be number one anymore."

Huh? If I leave, he'll be number one automatically.

"What are you talking about, Matt?"

"Don't play dumb."

Who's playing?

"Matt, I *really* don't know what you're talking about."

"Liar! Like you haven't noticed those meetings Dad's been going to."

I feel my hands curl into fists, angry because Matt called me a liar. Then I uncurl my fingers, thinking, I *am* a liar.

As Matt walks back to the house, I think about what he said. "You mean those school conferences with Mr. Arnt?" I call out. "What's that got to do with anything?"

The door slams behind him, so I don't get a reply. I stand there alone, shivering in the dark.

Busted and insulted, I think. And no tarp.

"Oh...no," I mumble as I walk back to the house. "And now I have to ride in that stupid parade."

2:40 P.M.

The embarrassment is huge. I'm the biggest kid riding a bike in the parade. And there are red, white, and blue

131

streamers tied to my handlebars and clickers on the spokes.

Booths are set up all around the square, selling sauerkraut and brats, dumplings and hot potato salad, apple cider and root beer. Mr. Lindholm and his wife wave at me, and Mr. Puffin is with them. All my teachers are there, too, even Mr. Arnt. I figure the entire county has turned out. When I pass the Quilt Circle booth, Lizzie and Mrs. Bixby run into the street, whistling at me.

I want to ride off the edges of the earth. As soon as I reach the end of the block, I rip the streamers off my Rover Sport. A familiar voice coming from behind makes me jump.

"If I didn't know better, I'd think you were avoiding me."

"Oh. How ya doin', Miss Peachcott? I've been busy, *real* busy. You know, with homework and chores and delivering pizza."

"Yes, I hear you've started a delivery business. That's why I needed to see you."

"It is?"

"You see, I'm crippled up." She holds her cane with its black rubber stop in front of my nose. "And we're nearing the winter solstice. You know what *that* means." She pauses, studying my face. "You do know what that means?"

I shake my head no.

"Means the days are getting shorter. You noticed that?"

I nod, even though I'm still confused.

"I need to dedicate my daylight hours to my formula," she continues. "My eyes are worn out—cataracts, you see. Makes things blurry. And Nova just returned the trial sample of my latest formula. They say I still don't have it right." She leans close. "I just made a new batch today. Can you see that birthmark?"

The spot on her face looks like it's throbbing. "Yes ma'am, I can see it."

"Blast!" She sighs. "So when can you start to work for me?"

"Well, what exactly would I be doing?"

"Why, delivering Nova so I can dedicate myself to my formula!"

More deliveries! I need money bad because, thanks to Matt, I've decided to give up scrounging for things. I didn't like being called a thief. Now I'll have to buy whatever else I need.

"So you want me to drop off Nova bags to your customers?"

"Yes, and pick up the money."

I can't believe it. She knows Mom's in jail, and she still trusts me. On the spot, I go from liking Elsie Peach-cott to loving her.

"Okay," I say. "Can I start right away?"

"Not so fast, buddy. How much you gonna charge a crippled-up old woman?"

Is she trying to make me feel bad so I'll work cheap? She is—she's haggling with me! I grin, remembering the way Mr. Lopez taught me to haggle with people in the markets across the border. "Never pay the asking price, Frankie Joe," he told me. "Dicker them down to *your* price."

"Well, depends on how far I have to travel," I say now. "Um, how about fifty cents per delivery inside the village limits...and a quarter a mile for out-of-town deliveries. That's what I charge Mr. Puffin and Mr. Lindholm—a quarter a mile."

Miss Peachcott looks thoughtful. "That's gonna add up."

It might, I think, but I'm running out of time.

"Well, you see," I tell her, "I got homework to do when I get home. And chores!" I suck the spit from between my teeth and shake my head slowly. "FJ won't let me work for you if I don't get my homework and chores done."

"He won't, huh?"

"No ma'am. And if Nova buys your formula, you'll be on easy street."

"That's true." She looks thoughtful. "Well, I guess we have a deal...*if—*"

Uh-oh.

"If...what?" I ask.

"*If* you'll agree to be my tester."

"Tester?"

"Yes, tester. Someone to tell me if I have got the formula right before I send it off to Nova again. They've given me only one more chance. I *must* get it right."

I helped Mr. Lopez mix his paint color. How hard can it be?

"Okay—"

"*And*," she interrupts, "if you help me dye my roots."

"Roots?"

Exasperated, Miss Peachcott parts her hair, exposing white roots below her black-licorice curls. Then she pulls a small brush from her pocketbook. "I use this slanted eye-shadow brush to dab color on the roots, you see, and my hands are not as steady as they once were."

Her hands *are* shaky.

"So," I say, taking a closer look at the black blotches on her scalp. Her hair dye is the blackest black I've ever seen, and her scalp is the whitest white. I can't decide which looks worse—the black blotches on her head or the throbbing blotch on her face. "You want me to deliver Nova...and be a tester and a dabber."

She blinks. "Yes, a tester and a dabber."

We shake hands on the deal.

7:30 P.M.

Pulling the dictionary from my bookshelf, I hunt up the new word I learned today.

sol-stice \ *noun* : **1** : either of the two points on the elliptic at which its distance from the celestial equator is greatest and which is reached by the sun each year about June 22 and December 22 **2** : the time of the sun's passing a solstice that occurs about June 22 to begin summer and December 22 to begin winter in the northern hemisphere.

Woo-hoo. Winter doesn't start until December 22. I have more time than I thought I did.

I close the dictionary, feeling good. Now that I'm working for Miss Peachcott *and* delivering pizzas, I can make the money I need long before then.

Friday, November 6

6:15 P.M.

Lizzie comes through the back door carrying an arm-load of shopping bags with JCPenney printed on the outside. As soon as we're through eating, she begins opening them.

"Try this on, Frankie Joe." She holds up a blue quilted parka with an attached hood. "Consider it an early Christmas present."

Cool. The jacket is just what I need for the trip.

I put on the jacket and stand for inspection, feeling a little bad because I'll only need it to get me back to Texas. It won't get any use once I get home.

"Perfect fit." Lizzie turns a smiling face to FJ and the four legitimate Huckaby boys. "Not too big and not too little, so he's got room to grow."

"Perfect," FJ echoes.

Huckaby Numbers Two, Three, Four, and Five do not reply. Nor do they smile.

Opening another of the shopping bags, Lizzie holds up funny-looking quilted pants with straps that go over the shoulders.

"Put the bibs on," Lizzie says, handing them to me. "They go over your other clothes."

"Now?"

"And try them with the jacket, too," Lizzie says. "I want to see if the entire outfit is the right size."

Uh-uh, I think. No way.

I don't move.

"Put them on," FJ says.

I read the unwritten rule in FJ's eyes that says, Do not argue with Lizzie. Taking off the jacket, I tug the pant straps over my shoulders and slip into the jacket again.

"Is that all?" Johnny asks, hunting through the empty bags. "How come we don't get new bibs?"

"The ones I bought you last year still fit you," Lizzie says. "I bought them big enough to last two years, remember?"

"But mine's got a hole in the knee," Johnny says.

"Your mom can patch them," FJ says. "Frankie Joe doesn't have any winter clothes, so we had to buy him some. Besides, we, uh, we've had some other unexpected expenses come up, so the rest of you will have to make do."

"That's right," Lizzie says, opening the last bag. "Now put these Wellingtons on, Frankie Joe. I need to see if they fit. I like to buy them big, too, so they'll last more than one year."

Wellingtons? I discover they're rubber boots that come almost to my knees. As soon as I have them on, she hands me mittens for my hands. Blue ones. I stand in front of my audience, feeling like the Michelin Man.

"And I got my fifteen-percent discount," Lizzie says to FJ. "Which will help a lot given the . . . circumstances."

Like what, I wonder. That my mom's in jail, and you had to take in an illegitimate son? And he's costing you more for food? And clothes? And fees for the after-school program?

"Looks like you're all set," FJ says to me. "Haul your new duds upstairs now. Your Responsibility Report's due Sunday. Better make sure it's caught up."

Responsibility Report—my seventh so far. I slump inside the new clothes. They're so new they don't bend, so I waddle out of the room in my "new duds."

Just as I'm about to go up the narrow stairs to the attic, I hear a whisper coming from behind me.

"Just 'cause you got new stuff, doesn't mean you'll be staying here," Matt says.

What's he freaking out over?

I don't know how to respond because Matt is talking in riddles. Little Johnny walks up, saving me the need.

" 'Cause of you, we didn't get early Christmas presents," he says, looking like he's about to cry. "I wish you didn't come here, Frankie Joe."

"Me too," I mutter, clumping up the stairs.

I feel ridiculous. Folks in Texas don't wear such things. I decide it doesn't matter. I'm planning on being gone soon, so I won't need them—except the jacket.

When I get to the attic, I peel off the clothes and pitch them onto the stack of boxes in the storage area. I feel bad. They probably cost a lot, and Little Johnny didn't get anything—not even a pair of mittens.

I only need the jacket, I think. I'll leave the bibs and boots and mittens for him. He'll grow into them.

Saturday, November 7

12:15 P.M.

Mr. Lopez would really like these colors. The leaves look like red and gold and yellow feathers floating in the air.

I sit on the front stoop watching kids race their bikes. I see Mandy in the street along with others from our fifth-grade class. They race through piles of leaves, making them swirl. It looks like a lot of fun.

The four brothers are inside the house, getting ready for their Saturday-afternoon events.

Maybe just once before I leave...

Deciding to make a run through the leaves, I haul my Rover Sport off the porch and ride to the end of the block.

"Hey, Oddball," Mandy says, riding with me to the start line. "Glad to see you're not hidin' out anymore."

I can't help but grin at the other oddball. But when I turn around to begin my run through the leaves, I find she's not the only one who will be riding along with me. One by one, our classmates line up on either side of us.

"They want you to race them," Mandy whispers.

Yeah, I got that.

"I'm not racing," I tell them. "I just wanna make one run through the leaves." I take off before anyone can answer.

Mandy takes off after me. They all take off.

Kids and bikes surround me. One kid behind me bumps my Rover Sport, so I pedal faster to get ahead of him. All at once, another kid pulls right in front of me.

"Move over!" I yell. "We're gonna crash!" He doesn't move, so I swerve to one side and begin to pump. When I near the finish line in front of the house, I lean forward, using my weight as momentum. I leave everything behind—trees and houses and bikers.

"Yahoo!" I yell, wheeling to a stop. The leaves swirl around me like I'm in the middle of a leaf tornado.

"You won!" Mandy yells, pulling up next to me. "You won the race!"

"I wasn't racing." Rolling my bike to the curb, I see the four brothers on the porch.

"Boy, Frankie Joe," Johnny calls out, "you're pretty fast!"

"*Real* fast," Luke says. "You beat those others by a mile."

"I can beat him," Matt growls. He pulls his bike off the porch and pushes it into the street.

"I don't know." Mark sounds doubtful. "Frankie Joe

beat me in that race, remember? And he's even faster on his bike."

"Shut up," Mandy tells Mark. "Let them race. Just once, I'd like to see someone put Matt in his place."

All the kids start yelling, "Race! Race!"

"I'm ready," Matt says, pulling his bike up next to mine. "Let's get to the starting line."

I look at the racing tires on Matt's bike. I don't stand a chance against those tires. "I'm not gonna race you," I tell him. "I just wanted to make one run."

"I dare you," Matt says.

"No."

"Double dare you!"

"No." I'm not about to give Matt, the honor student and Student Council representative, another chance to rub it in.

Matt blows up like a bag of microwave popcorn. "You're chicken!" he yells, turning to the other kids. "Scared Sneaky Freaky Slow Frankie Joe's a chicken!"

Everyone's yells, "Scared Sneaky Freaky Slow Frankie Joe's chicken."

I can't take it. Before I know it, I'm racing back down the street. I hear the others behind me, yelling "He's gonna race! He's gonna race Matt!"

Are they going to be surprised. They think I'm heading for the starting line, but I'm not.

When I reach the cornfield at the end of the block,

I don't stop. I race down a corn row without slowing down. The long leaves slap me in the face, and I bounce over the roots; but I don't look back. I know that no one will follow me because their skinny tires aren't right for off-road biking.

Only a little longer, I think, letting the corn swallow me up. Soon I'll leave this one-horse town in my dust.

9:47 P.M.

Delivering pizzas has made me tired, but before bed, I revise my escape-to-Texas plan again.

Bedroll Got it.

Tarp Have to buy one.

Spare bike tube and flat kit Buy at the
    garage downtown.

Pot for cooking Got it.

Matches to start a fire Maybe in the kitchen.

Canteen Use plastic bottles.

Jacket Got one.

Bungee cord Got it.

Money Working on it.

Triple A maps Got them.

Mementos Can't leave them behind.

"Wait," I mumble. "I'll need a change of clothes for when I wash out my dirty ones in the rivers." I add a pair of jeans and shirt, socks and underwear to my list and look it over again. I decide to make a quick run downstairs to check out matches. On the ground floor, I wait, listening to see if Matt's following me.

The coast is clear.

I inch my way down the hall but stop at the kitchen door. Someone's talking.

Swell. FJ and Lizzie are still up. I stand quiet, listening.

"How long you think it'll take?" Lizzie asks.

"He wasn't sure," FJ answers. "Four to six months, I figure."

"That long?"

"These kind of things don't happen overnight," he says.

"You think there'll be any...problems?"

Silence.

Wonder what problems they're worried about?

I sneak my way back down the hall and up the stairs. I have my own problems. December 22—when winter begins—is a little over a month away, and I still don't have everything I need.

Saturday, November 21

1:20 P.M.

I'm racing to Mr. Puffin's farm with a large pepperoni-and-sausage pizza when I hear a grumbling that sounds like a giant growling dog. As I get closer, I see dirt swirling into the sky. Under the dust, I can make out farm equipment. The tractors and harvesters and trucks that were parked inside the red barns are in the fields now.

Like giant insects, the harvesters devour corn and soybeans. The machines shoot yellow kernels into the back of big trucks with tall sideboards that keep the grain from falling out. Truck after truck loaded with shelled corn and soybeans leave the fields. I can't believe it. In the blink of an eye, the ground is barren as a brown paper bag. Just like the Chihuahua Desert.

My plan has developed a huge case of the hiccups. I start pedaling again and make it to Mr. Puffin's back door just as the old farmer is coming in from the fields.

"Perfect timing," he says, removing the insulated bag from my basket. "I done worked up an appetite. Let's have a slice while it's good and hot."

Wordless, I follow Mr. Puffin into his kitchen. Pocketing the money he hands me, I watch him plate up pizza. I stare at my slice. How can I eat pizza when giant shredders are ripping apart my escape-to-Texas plan?

Mr. Puffin looks at me. "You tired of pizza? I got some peanut butter and jelly, you want a sandwich."

"No sir, it's just—they're cutting down the corn and beans! They're taking *everything*. The cornstalks and bean plants and...there's nothing left."

"You've never seen a harvest before, have you, Frankie Joe? You see, we got equipment these days that shells the corn and beans right off the stalk, then takes the stalks down to the ground. Well, almost to the ground. There's a little stalk and root left to the corn. Roots rot, making fertilizer for next year's crop. Cornstalks are chopped up, made into silage to feed cows. Farmers sell off the shelled corn and beans, or put them in storage until prices are better."

Storage. I'd forgotten about the big blue silos.

"Oh sure. The corn and beans are stored in those Harvestore silos."

I begin to breathe easy again. I can get food out of the silos when I need it. I still have to figure out a way to hide if I need to, but at least I'll have plenty to eat.

Mr. Puffin shakes his head. "Silos are for storing

silage. Or used to be. You see, not too many farmers raise dairy cows anymore. Most silos just sit empty now. Lot of the barns, too."

"You mean silos are for storing food for *cows*?"

"That's right. Corn and beans are hauled straight to river barges—that'd be on the Mississippi River for us here—or straight to the processing plants."

"But don't farmers save back enough for themselves?"

"Themselves? Oh, you mean those that feed their own livestock. Don't feed corn and beans to dairy cows. Feed silage."

I shake my head. "No sir, for *eating*. You know, corn and beans for making things like...burritos."

He laughs. "Why, don't eat none of it, son! We grow field corn, not sweet corn. Field corn's tough, not that tasty. What we grow is processed for other things. Lot of what we grow 'round here goes for ethanol."

"Eth–a...*what*?"

"Ethanol! You know. Gasoline."

I fall back in my chair. "Corn is made into gasoline? But—but this is the Bread Basket of the World."

Mr. Puffin helps himself to another slice of pizza. "That's right, it is. Wheat and oats, barley and rye are still grown for human consumption. Corn, too, other places. But most of what we grow here is not the eatable kind.

"Big changes in farming nowadays," he goes on. "Not like it was back in the last century. When my grandpa came here, was nothing but tall-grass prairies. Grass grew taller than a man's head. Now *corn* grows taller than a man's head and is turned into fuel for cars. By the time you're growed up, probably be using corn to fly rocket ships to one of them planets out there." He points upward. "How about it, Frankie Joe? You thinking of turnin' corn into fuel for rocket ships?"

"No sir, I was thinking of eating it."

"Oh, can't be doing that. Crops are treated with pesticides and insecticides to keep the molds down and kill the bugs." He eyes me. "You been eatin' the stuff that grows 'round here?"

"No sir."

My slice of pizza has gotten cold, but I don't notice. I'm imagining myself hiding out in country barren as the moon and glowing in the dark like a radioactive mutant because I have nothing to eat but chemical-tainted corn and soybeans.

Mr. Puffin gets up from the table. "Gotta get back outside. Need to get my equipment in the barn before it gets too late."

I follow him out the door.

"Better wear this wool jacket home," he tells me as I climb onto my bike. He points to a thermometer hanging on the side of his back door. It reads thirty-two degrees.

The freezing point of water, I remember.

"Thanks. I'll return it soon as I can."

Mr. Puffin looks toward the horizon. "Well now, look at that. I swear that looks like an Alberta clipper comin' in." He looks at me. "And you know what that means."

I eye the blue-gray sky beyond the colorless fields. "No sir. What does that mean?"

He grins. "It means I can drive into town now and eat my pizza at Gambino's. It's time to close down shop for the year. No more work to do."

No more work? But I don't have enough money yet!

"But—but what about your cows? You need to milk them morning and night."

Mr. Puffin laughs. "Where's your head, son? You mean you rode right past the barn and never noticed them cows are gone? I decided to take your daddy's advice. Sold every one of those Holsteins. Got a good price, too." He smiles at me. "No cows to milk, and the crops are outta the field. Lookin' at them clouds, I'd say it's in the nick a time. No need to have my pizza delivered anymore. Least not until next spring when the seed goes into the ground."

He helps me slip into the jacket, and I ride slowly back to town, looking at fields the color of a brown paper bag.

3:10 P.M.

The Saturday Quilt Circle is still meeting when I get back. I try to slip past the roomful of chattering women, but I don't make it.

"Sit down next to me," Mrs. Bixby says. "I'll quiz you on your multiplication tables. You still need to learn to count by sevens."

I stifle a groan. "I *know* how to count by sevens."

"You do? Well then, show us. Recite your sevens."

"Now?"

"Now," Lizzie says.

I moan silently, then recite sevens clear up to seven times thirty. The women in the Quilt Circle smile. Lizzie beams.

"I taught him that," Mrs. Bixby says, looking pleased. "Well then, time to move on to eights."

I moan loud this time. "But I was gonna go upstairs and look up something in my dictionary."

"Oh? Well, no need to go upstairs." Mrs. Bixby pulls a dictionary out of her quilt bag.

Of course. She carries one with her. I turn the pages quickly and read silently.

Al-ber-ta clip-per \ *noun* : a severe storm, often with a heavy snowfall, coming from Alberta, Canada, and the Canadian Rocky Mountains and swiftly moving east and southeast across the USA's Midwest.

But it's not time for snow. It's only November!

"You feeling all right?" Lizzie brushes her fingers across my forehead.

"He is looking a little peaked," an old quilter with white hair murmurs.

"Indeed," another one says.

"Oh, nothing wrong with him," Mrs. Bixby says. "He just needs to practice his eights."

"No, I think he needs to rest," Lizzie says. "He's been working real hard."

Wordless, I head for the stairs.

"Wait," Mrs. Bixby calls out. "Now that you're working, you can buy a raffle ticket."

"Oh, I don't think that's necessary," Lizzie says.

Mrs. Bixby frowns. "Why Lizzie, we had a thousand tickets printed up and have lots of them left. Don't forget, the raffle helps fund The Great Escape. Besides, what's he doing with all that money he's making?"

Lizzie blinks, then looks at me.

I buy a ticket.

Monday, November 23

6:20 A.M.

Snow! *Lots* of snow! The Alberta clipper blew in like a Texas tornado last night, burying everything in fluffy, white, *cold* snow. The house shook from the windblasts. Though Lizzie gave me two more blue-ribbon quilts, my teeth chattered as I lay in bed.

Finally it's morning. Even though the days have gotten shorter, and it's still dark outside, I can see a white blanket through the attic windows, covering everything.

I'm excited until I realize what it means. My delivery business is doomed.

At breakfast Lizzie asks, "Where are your new clothes and boots?" I look around the kitchen table and see the four brothers are dressed in bibs. Then I look at the coatrack at the back door and see four parkas. In the boot tray are four pairs of Wellingtons.

FJ gives me his look, and I go to get into my new duds.

7:45: A.M.

Walking to school, I see a plow pushing snow to the curb along the street and people shoveling sidewalks. I pick up a handful of snow, shape it into a ball, and throw it against the side of a building. My first snowball! I make another, then another.

I wish my school friends in Laredo were here. They've never seen snow either. We could make a snow fort—and have a snowball fight!

I debate skipping school altogether so I can play in the snow, but I have a test in Math today. As I turn toward school, I notice other kids in similar clothes, looking like miniature Technicolor versions of the Michelin Man.

Mandy's coat and pants are strawberry pink. "Hey," she says, waddling up next to me. The snow is knee-deep for her. "Don't walk so fast," she complains. "In case you haven't noticed, my legs aren't as long as yours."

"What's that stuff the snowplows are putting on the street?" I ask, slowing down.

"Cinders and sand. It helps the snow melt and gives the tires traction."

Cool. At least I can still deliver Nova for Miss Peachcott.

Saturday, November 28

7:15 A.M.

It's *so* depressing, I think, looking out the attic window. Everywhere, white...white...white. Another clipper blew in during the night, dumping six more inches of snow. One more thing to interfere with my escape plan. No corn to hide out in. Nothing to eat along the way. Snowdrifts too big to bike through. I almost yearn to see soybean green again.

Every day this week has been the same. Snowplows wake me early, growling their way up and down the streets. I leave for school in the dark and come home in the dark, slipping and sliding on sidewalks covered with chunky ice. I like making snowballs and snowmen when the snow is soft, but now there's an icy crust on the top, making it hard. The snowplows pile dirty snow everywhere, and I have to take turns shoveling the front porch and sidewalk.

But then I smile, remembering that today is different. Today is my first day as tester and dabber.

I decide to take Mr. Lopez's paint memento to show Miss Peachcott. The treads on my Rover Sport's fat tires grab onto the cinders and sand without much sliding, just as they do on desert hardpan. And even though I don't like them, my Michelin-Man jacket and pants keep me warm.

"Come in, Frankie Joe," Miss Peachcott says when I wade through the knee-deep snow to her door. "I've got your deliveries all sacked up. But we have other business to tend to first."

I peel out of my parka and boots and sit down. A box of Girl Scout cookies is on the kitchen table. Shortbread.

"Help yourself to a cookie while I set up." She pauses as she's gathering things. "And tell me when that jackrabbit mother of yours gets out of jail."

I knew it! I knew she'd ask! I chew on a cookie for a long time, considering how much to tell her. Just the good stuff, I decide.

"Um, Mom gets out in July, but she's talking to a lawyer about a new hearing. She's thinking about going into business with her new friends, so I figure that will work in her favor. It shows she's being enterprising."

"Business?" She frowns. "What kind of business?"

"I dunno. She didn't say."

"Oh my, I hope she's not chasing rainbows."

Rainbows again. I feel my shoulders droop.

"There's lots of things she can do," I say. "She's worked all kinds of jobs before—in clothes stores and cafés and even a hardware store once. And I'll help her in her new business. Maybe I'll do deliveries for her."

She looks surprised. "You're planning on going back to Texas?"

"Well sure, why wouldn't I? Mom needs me. I help her out a lot."

She hesitates. "Well now, it's just that you seem to be settling in here so well. I'm sure Frank and Lizzie would hate to see you go."

I don't say anything.

"Is she coming to get you? Or is Frank planning to drive you back?"

Enough questions. I don't want to slip up and say something about my escape plan. "Maybe we better get started. I have lots of homework."

Miss Peachcott sits still as a stone as I work the black dye into white root hairs with the slanted eye-shadow brush. Stepping back, I survey my work.

Not one smudge.

My job as dabber done, we turn to testing colors. I pull Mr. Lopez's paint sample from my backpack and show it to Miss Peachcott.

"Why, the man has real talent! I've never seen such unique colors."

"He let me help mix this one—and name it."

"Very nice blue, not too overpowering. What did you name it?"

"Blue Moon, like the ice cream. It's one of my favorite flavors. It tastes like bubble gum."

"Oh? I've never had that flavor." She looks at the paint swatches again. "You think there's one here I can use?" She points to a shade of pink. "This one is pretty."

"Too dark," I say, considering the color. I look around the room for a closer match. "This is the color of your skin." I hold a Nova bag next to her face so she can see it in the mirror.

"Why, so it is. I'll see if I can duplicate it." She mixes and mashes creams and powders together, then smears a dab on her birthmark.

"How's that?"

"Um, now it's more the color of a raspberry."

She sighs. "I have spent a good bit of time with color theory, but the birthmark makes it difficult."

We work our way through various colors: peaches, red grapes, ripe plums. We're trying apple colors now.

"How'd I do this time?"

I hold a Nova bag up next to her latest creation. "I think you used too much red. It's the color of a flamingo."

"Blast!" Miss Peachcott throws the Nova bag on the floor. "It must be the dyes that Nova is providing me. I could do better using food coloring from the grocery store."

As she cleans the latest concoction off her face, I notice the more she takes off, the smaller the birthmark seems to get. I begin to think that she's making it more noticeable with her creations.

"Um, you ever think of not putting anything on it? I mean, no makeup at all on that spot."

Her eyes go round. "I'm a beauty consultant! A beauty consultant cannot have a blemish on her face. People would have no confidence in me if I let that birthmark show."

I consider this. "Well then, you ever think of having it cut off? I had a wart on my hand cut off once—a big one." I show her the scar on my hand. "Maybe they can cut that birthmark off."

She examines my scar. "I cannot have my skin puckering up that way! Why, my nose wouldn't sit straight on my face if I had that birthmark cut off."

She walks to the oven, which serves as her pantry, and takes out a package of food coloring. "Maybe I *will* give this a try."

I slip into my parka and boots. "I need to do your deliveries."

"Yes, yes, go on," she says, waving me toward the door. "I have work to do."

I feel a hollowness fill my chest as I wade through snow to my bike. I'm beginning to think that Miss Peachcott is the one who's chasing rainbows.

9:05 A.M.

Mrs. Brown is cooking breakfast when I knock on her back door.

"Oh, come in," she says when she sees the Nova bag in my hand. "Elsie said you would be handling deliveries." I stand at the back door to keep from dripping on her floor, but she waves me toward a chair. "You'll have to wait until I'm done here. Can't let breakfast burn."

Sitting down, I watch her fry sausages. According to Miss Peachcott, Mrs. Brown was skinny as a beanpole before her husband died. Now the square lump of a woman looks more like the entire bean patch.

"The doctor didn't say a word about my weight," she says, seeming to read my mind. "He just told me I needed to lower my cholesterol. You know anything about cholesterol, Frankie Joe?"

"Only what I see on the TV. I, uh, I think you're supposed to watch what you eat. You know, vegetables and fruits instead of fried foods?"

"I saw that, too. But I always fixed sausage and eggs for my husband, and he never put on a pound." She breaks three eggs into the frying pan. "I know he's gone, but I still fix the same breakfast. Five sausages and three eggs, over easy. And... well, waste not want not."

She turns to me, smiling. "How about you help me

out this morning. You need to eat hearty food in the winter to keep warm."

"Guess I could do that." I have noticed I'm hungrier than usual since the snows started. As I put away three of the sausages and two of the eggs, Mrs. Brown talks.

"I'm sure the medicine the doctor's put me on will help." She hesitates. "Say, do you make deliveries for people other than Elsie? You know, like prescriptions from the pharmacy? I'm not as steady as I used to be when I was lighter on my feet. Especially in all this snow."

"Sure! It's fifty cents a delivery."

We work out a schedule.

12:15 P.M.

The newlywed Mrs. Barnes is my last delivery of the day. She gave birth to twin girls a few weeks ago. When she invites me into the kitchen, the smell almost knocks me down. The mix of burned toast and dirty diapers and baby burp is overpowering. Right off, she shows me her twin daughters.

"My little twofers," she calls the two bundles wrapped in pink blankets. "I got two for the price of one."

"Just like at the pizza parlor," I say, eyeing the babies.

"Why, that's right." She laughs. "Used to be, I thought pizza was the only thing that came two for the price of one."

"Yes ma'am. Nothing better than two pepperoni pizzas on a Friday night."

"I remember." She pauses. "Gee, that seems like such a long time ago."

As the tired-looking woman begins to droop, I pull up chair so she can sit down. Before I know it, she's crying.

"It's just that I'm so tired," she says, blowing her nose in a tissue. "Do you know I average three hours of sleep a night?" She looks at me, her eyes liquid. "I never changed a diaper before the twins came...or had baby spit all over me...or cooked!" Her eyes begin to flood again.

I push the tissue box closer.

"I use to smell like Nova cologne. Now I smell of baby poop and burp and burned food. If I'm not standing in front of a stove, I'm trundling the twins to the store for groceries and detergent."

I feel as helpless as the pink bundles in the crib.

Lowering her head to the table, she says, "Lord help me, I don't know what I'd do if I ran out of detergent. All this snow just makes it harder to get to the store."

Something flashes in my mind. "I got an idea, Mrs. Barnes! I run a delivery business, you know—just fifty cents a trip. If I pick up things for you, maybe you could take a nap."

"Oh, what a wonderful idea!"

"And I could even bring you two pizzas on Friday nights."

She wipes her nose and smiles at me.

This enterprising business is easy, I think, wading through the snow back to my bike.

Saturday, December 12

11:45 A.M.

The letter is postmarked December 5. Mom mailed it a week ago.

Dear Frankie Joe,

I was real glad to hear from you. I am SO bored.

I knew about the four half brothers, FJ told me when I called him to come get you. Guess I forgot to mention it. I'm glad you have your own room. I have no privacy in this joint.

No news yet from the lawyer but he was optimistic. Ricky talked with him, too. I guess I'm over my mad at Ricky.

My new friends still want me to go into business with them. Don't know what yet. One gal's got this friend who has the scoop on something big. They are a lot of fun. One gal is from New Jersey. Boy does she talk funny. And another one is from

Las Vegas. She used to deal cards at one of those casinos! She's showing me how to deal like the professionals do.

My friends were set up, too, just like me. None of us belongs in here.

I'll write when I know more.

Love ya,

Marti

XOXOXO

FJ's sitting on the bed, watching me. I hand the letter to him to read before he asks. I can't afford to raise his suspicions now.

He reads the letter fast, then hands it back to me. "You need any more stamps...envelopes?"

"No sir. I got plenty, especially since Mom's gonna get out early."

He hesitates. "I wouldn't count on her getting out before her sentence is up."

"Why not?"

"It's not her first offense"—he hesitates, rubbing at his mouth—"and it sounds like she's making big plans."

"Right," I say hotly. "She's being enterprising!"

He gives his head a little shake. "Martha Jane was always one to chase rainbows."

Aargh. Now *he's* talking about rainbows.

"She's not chasing rainbows!"

He gives his head another shake. "A lot can happen between now and then, Frankie Joe."

It already has, I think. It snowed too early, so I can't leave until the snow melts. I begin to wonder just when that will be.

Mr. Puffin would know.

As FJ turns to leave, he looks around the attic. "You, uh, you doin' okay up here? You want, I can move those boxes to the storage shed. Need to get rid of a lot of this stuff anyway."

No! He'll find my escape box if he does that.

"That's okay," I say quickly. "I mean, I got plenty of room... and, uh, the storage shed is all snowed in."

"That's true. Well, okay then. When it warms up, we'll get things cleared out and give the place a fresh coat of paint. In the meantime, you can be thinking about what color you'd like it painted. Okay?"

"Sure." All these lies make my insides feel moldy, like I have smut balls inside me.

1:10 P.M.

The off-road tires on my Rover Sport are perfect for the slushy mix of rain and snow that falls early this afternoon. The legitimate Huckabys stored their bikes in the storage shed when the first Alberta clipper came through. But not me.

"Yoo-hoo, Frankie Joe."

I slow down, recognizing one of the women from the Quilt Circle. "Um, how are you doing, Mrs...."

"Wilkins. I'm Mrs. Wilkins. Remember?"

I nod.

"How lucky we ran into each other. I need to talk business with you."

"What kind of business?"

"Delivery business. Now that winter's here, I thought you could pick up groceries for me on Saturday mornings. I can call in the order ahead of time."

A new customer!

"Sure! I charge a fee."

"Elsie Peachcott told me. Fifty cents a delivery, I believe?"

"Yes ma'am. You wanna start tomorrow?"

"Indeed. Oh, and my neighbor Mr. Perkins thought you could do some errands for him, too. He's on a walker, you know. I'll introduce you to him when you bring my groceries by. Now I must get out of this weather. It's freezing out here. See you tomorrow."

It *is* freezing—colder than freezing. The temperature drops below thirty-two degrees all the time now. But I don't let the cold interfere with my delivery service. Or snow or ice. And my quilted clothes and Wellington boots keep me plenty warm.

Which is good because my business is really growing. Miss Peachcott. Mrs. Brown. Mrs. Barnes. And now Mrs. Wilkins and Mr. Perkins.

I start pedaling again. I'm going to Gambino's Pizza Parlor, hoping Mr. Puffin is there. The muscles in my legs feel like cords of steel when I pump the pedals up and down. My lungs don't even burn anymore when I breathe in the cold Canadian air. The slivers of ice that fall off the knotty tree limbs don't hurt my face, either, because my skin has weathered, like tough leather.

Just like Mr. O'Hare's, I think. Thinking of him makes me wish I were in the desert with him today, hunting space rocks.

Soon I think. Soon.

"Frankie Joe!" Mr. Puffin says as I walk into the pizza parlor. "Pull up a chair and have some pizza with me. I been missin' you. I ordered a twofer, so we can have a whole one each, you want."

"I better have just have one slice. Lizzie's fixing supper right now. And I came to see you about—" I think fast. How can I get the information I need without spilling the beans about my escape plan? I eye the pizza in front of me.

Of course! Talk about our business deal.

"I came to find out when you'll need me to start delivering pizza again. Last time I saw you, you said something about planting seed in the spring."

"That's right."

"So when do you do that...*exactly*?"

"Well now, depends on when the soil's warm enough. I like to get mine in the ground early—before the rains begin. Seeds need water to sprout, you see. Late March usually, maybe first of April."

"So the snow should be gone by the end of March?"

"About then, yeah."

My new escape date.

Friday, December 18

5:10 P.M.

"What'cha get Mama and Daddy for Christmas?"

Little Johnny is standing at the top of the stairs, his hands behind his back and his eyes sparkling.

Oh no. I glance at the calendar on the wall. Christmas is only a week away.

"Nothing...yet. What did you get them?"

"You have to promise me that you'll keep it a secret."

Secret? When did Johnny decide I was trustworthy? Maybe when I became the tiebreaker?

"Okay, I promise."

"Gloves!" Huckaby Number Five pulls two pairs of knit gloves from behind his back. One large brown pair for FJ, one smaller blue pair for Lizzie.

I finger the soft yarn. "These are nice. Where'd you get them?"

"At the gift shop."

"The one we walk past it on the way home from school?"

"Yep, they have lots of gifts at the gift shop."

"That makes sense," I say, grinning. "How much you pay for these gloves? For the two pair?"

"Five dollars each. That's...that's—"

I finish the calculation for him. "Ten dollars."

"Plus tax. I took three five-dollar bills out of my savings, and I got money back." He pulls money from his pocket to show me.

"Your savings? Wow! Where'd you get so much money?"

"Dad sets up a Christmas Club account every year for us. He puts money in it every month...." He pauses. "Only he told us he had to cut back this year 'cause there'll be five accounts now, and he's got other 'spenses."

Great. Now I'm the Grinch that stole Christmas.

Johnny adds, "I gotta wrap them up today 'cause we're decorating the tree tomorrow, and I gotta put them under it."

Tree? I forgot.

"What'd you get them?" Johnny repeats.

"Um, nothing yet. You better leave now so I can go shopping, okay?"

He smiles. "Okay."

"You think I can get two gifts for ten dollars, too?"

"Sure. They have lots of stuff on sale 'cause Christmas is gettin' close. The lady there gave me a deal on my gloves. She's real nice."

He leans close and begins to whisper even though there's no one to hear us. "Let's put our stuff under the tree together, okay? It'll be our secret."

Our secret. If Johnny knew the real secret I was keeping, I bet it wouldn't stay secret long.

5:30 P.M.

I reach the gift shop just thirty minutes before it closes. The store is a Christmas fairyland, with packages of spicy teas in colorful boxes, chocolates stuffed with cherries, and trays of jewelry that sparkle red and green.

"You need help, Frankie Joe?" A thin, silver-haired woman at the counter smiles at me.

I look at her curiously. "You know my name?"

"Well, of course," she laughs. "Everyone in town knows *your* name. You're that enterprising Huckaby boy that started a delivery service."

I feel my face turn warm. Sometimes I just want to yell out the reason I'm being so enterprising.

"My name's Ellen Thompson," she says. "You look around all you want."

"I guess I'll take these," I tell her a few minutes later. I hold out two fleece scarves I've picked up off a counter.

One blue floral and one brown plaid. The scarves cost five dollars each, so I hand her three fives. "They're for FJ and Lizzie."

"Oh, your parents are just gonna love these! And I know they'll get a lot of use from them, too. This winter's turning out to be a doozy."

Your parents? The words sting like ice pellets. Lizzie is not my mother, I want to say. And FJ is like a warden.

Mrs. Thompson hands me four dollar bills and thirty cents in change. But before I can take the change, she closes her fingers around it.

"Oh wait!" she says, her forehead squeezing into wrinkles. "What about your brothers?"

Brothers? They're mutants, I think, and I don't want to buy them anything. All I want is my change back.

"I know—chocolate-covered pretzels!" Without warning she pulls four chocolate-covered pretzels from a jar on the counter.

I look at the price on the jar: Fifty cents each. "But that's not enough money—"

"Well now, I think it's just enough."

Before I can blink, the coins disappear into the cash till. My escape money is disappearing faster than snowdrifts in front of a snowplow.

"I'll just gift wrap all this up for you." She smiles an extraordinarily big smile. "No charge."

As she tears Christmas paper off a big roll, I

remember something important. I haven't gotten Mom anything for Christmas. As Mrs. Thompson wraps the presents, I walk around the shop.

Mom won't need scarves or earmuffs or gloves in Texas. And I don't have enough money for expensive things, like wall plaques and teapots and coffeemakers... unless I spend more of my escape money.

What should I do? Buy Mom a nice gift? Or save my money so I can be waiting when she gets out of jail?

I decide that Christmas just wouldn't be Christmas without a package to open. Especially for someone in jail. I pick up a bag of potpourri—a mix of dried flower petals and scented berries—that would make her cell smell nice. The price on the package is marked ten dollars.

Ten dollars! Quickly I do the math, figuring how many deliveries I would need to make to earn that much. Ten dollars divided by fifty cents is twenty. Twenty deliveries to buy Mom a present, unless...

"All finished, Frankie Joe."

I look at Mrs. Thompson, wondering if she would cut a deal for "that enterprising Huckaby boy." I decide to try dickering her down to *my* price. Five dollars and not a penny more.

"Thanks," I say as I take the bag holding my packages. "I'll be back tomorrow. I, uh, I need a gift for someone else, too."

"Oh?"

I can read the curiosity in Mrs. Thompson's eyes, but I leave the shop without answering. Some secrets can't be trusted to anyone. Especially in a one-horse town like Clearview.

Saturday, December 19

3:25 P.M.

I sneak past the Saturday Quilt Circle. Since I've started my delivery business, Lizzie has given me a reprieve from Saturday tutoring. But I know if Mrs. Bixby sees me, I'm doomed. I need to get to the gift shop so I can buy Mom a Christmas present. I pause, trying to remember which board on the landing is the squeaky one.

Creak. Wrong one.

Mrs. Bixby is in the front hallway in a flash. "Stop right there, Frankie Joe," she says. Her eyes are extra fidgety.

The rest of the Quilt Circle troop is behind her. Including Lizzie. The entire group stares at me as if an expectation hasn't been met.

Mrs. Bixby says, "Well?"

I look to Lizzie for a translation.

"The village president drew for the quilt." Lizzie's voice sounds hoarse, and her eyes are round as quarters.

"And no one's claimed it yet. The winning number is 7–7–7."

7–7–7. My heart is pounding. I bolt upstairs.

"Where'd I put it?" I look inside my book from Mrs. Jones, and the one from Mr. O'Hare. Then I remember that I'm using the raffle ticket for a bookmark in my dictionary. Pulling it out quickly, I read 7 . . . 7 . . . 7.

"I won," I whisper. Then I start yelling, "I won I won I won!"

Clear from the first floor, I hear the Quilt Circle calling out, "He won! He won!" The stairs creak, and I see that Lizzie has climbed all the way to the attic.

"Oh, Frankie Joe," she says, rushing to me. "I'm so happy for you. Do I need to guess who you're giving it to?"

For a second, I wonder if she thinks I'm giving it to her. Then I decide that's a dopey idea because Lizzie has closets full of blue-ribbon quilts. So I just grin.

"I knew it! Martha Jane's getting a handmade quilt from home. It's just the *perfect* Christmas present." She smothers me with a hug.

Yeah, it *is* perfect. Now I can save my escape money to give Mom the best present of all.

Me.

4:25 P.M.

Lizzie helps me package the quilt for mailing. The squares of soybean green and corn gold look like an aerial photograph of Clearview, Illinois.

"This will be a good remembrance," Lizzie says. "Don't you think so, FJ?"

He's sitting at the table, writing out an address label for the package. "Real nice remembrance," he says.

Remembrance. That's a new word for me. It sounds like a nice word, but did Lizzie's eyes look sad when she said it? I file the word away to check on later.

Lizzie brings out a box of Christmas cards. "Pick out one for your mother," she tells me. "And if you like, take some for other friends you'd like to send cards to."

FJ pulls a ten-dollar bill from his wallet. "This should cover postage for the package. Post office closes soon. Better hurry."

I look at the money that FJ hands me. It doesn't feel right that he should have to pay to mail Mom's present.

"Thanks," I say, "but I'll use my own money." I pick out four cards and rush upstairs.

Watch the mail for a present, I write in Mom's card. *Be seeing you soon! XOXOXO.* I address the card to her in care of the Webb County Texas Jail.

I write the same thing in cards to Mrs. Jones, Mr. O'Hare, and Mr. Lopez: *I'll be coming to see you soon. Keep an eye out for me. Your friend, Frankie Joe Huckaby.* I address their cards in care of the Lone Star Trailer Park, Laredo, Texas.

Making a dash down the stairs, I put the package and cards into my bike basket and head for the post office. It's five minutes before closing when I burst through the door.

"My goodness, Frankie Joe," the postmaster says, looking startled. "What's your hurry?"

"Need to get this package to Texas by Christmas Day," I say, breathless.

"Let me check the zone." She looks at the zip code on the package and checks a chart. "Oh my goodness, I need to hold the truck!"

I watch as she races to the back door.

She's smiling when she comes back. "Good thing you weren't five minutes later. If the package leaves today, it should have a good chance of reaching Laredo by Christmas."

"And these cards, too?" I hand her the four Christmas cards.

"I'll get them on the truck as well."

"Thanks," I say.

Now everyone will know that I'm coming home soon.

7:25 P.M.

The front room smells like pine air freshener. The Christmas tree is huge, the biggest tree I've ever seen. FJ strings lights around it, and the tree twinkles like a thousand stars. Lizzie pops corn, and we make strings out of it. Then we do the same thing with cranberries. Because I'm taller, I hang glass balls on the upper branches, and my half brothers fill in the middle and bottom.

"What do you think, Frankie Joe?" Lizzie asks, standing back to admire the tree.

"It's the first real Christmas tree I've ever seen. My Mom thinks Christmas trees are a waste of money. But Mrs. Jones lets me help decorate her artificial tree every year."

"Artificial ones are nice too—and almost as real-looking as a live one," says Lizzie.

"Sounds like you have nice friends back there," FJ says.

"Yes sir, the best."

"It's time, Frankie Joe." Johnny grins as he pulls his Christmas gifts from behind his back.

"Oh yeah." I run upstairs and bring mine down. I place my six wrapped gifts next to Johnny's.

Lizzie beings to cry.

The brothers are speechless when they see that they have presents, too.

"That was real nice, Frankie Joe," FJ tells me, putting his hand on my shoulder.

I wish it had been my idea.

9:45 P.M.

Just before lights-out, I look up a new word in my dictionary.

re-mem-brance \ noun : a memory of a person, thing, or event.

I crawl into the squeaky metal bed underneath the window that looks onto the snowy backyard. But in my mind's eye, I'm seeing a different scene: one with cactus and sagebrush and colored like a brown paper bag....

All at once, it's last year, and I'm back at the Lone Star Trailer Park. Mom is waiting for a friend to pick her up to go dancing. She's wearing her new blouse with fringe on the sleeves and her red cowgirl boots. "Come on," she says, "I'll teach you to line dance." We laugh as I try to follow her feet. When we hear a car horn outside, she tells me not to wait up for her. "You forgot again," I yell as she races out the front door. "I'm staying over at Mrs. Jones's tonight, remember?" She gives me a wave, and I head for Mrs. Jones's trailer.

I love helping Mrs. Jones decorate her tree. Her ornaments are fun because she made them herself. Fuzzy snowflakes crocheted out of white yarn. Tin drums made out of Vienna sausage cans she glued felt on. Toy soldiers made from wooden clothespins she painted red and blue. Mr. O'Hare always comes, too, since he doesn't have a family like Mr. Lopez. Like always, he brings a fruitcake he bought at Felipe's. After we finish decorating the tree, Mrs. Jones heats apple cider in a pot on the stove, and we eat fruitcake, which I pretend to like....

A remembrance, I think. I'm having a remembrance. I feel warm all over.

But as my eyes grow heavy, a question slips into my half-asleep, half-awake mind. Why would such a nice word make Lizzie look sad?

Friday, December 25

7:45 A.M.

Early Christmas morning, Lizzie calls to me from the bottom of the stairs. "Your mom's on the phone. Hurry down!"

I'm downstairs in two shakes. When I reach the kitchen, I hear FJ talking.

"...and he's doing real well in school, too, making giant strides." He glances my way. "Wait, he's here now. I'll put him on." He hands me the phone. "She can't talk long, and the reception's poor."

I'm so breathless, I can hardly talk. "Hi Mom, did you get the package?"

"Yes I did! The quilt is beautiful! It got here yesterday."

"You like it? The Quilt Circle made it."

"Well of course I like it. It's amazing."

"It would probably win a blue ribbon at the county fair."

She laughs. "They still have those things? Tell me, how could you afford such a pretty thing? It looks expensive."

"Oh no. Two dollars is all the ticket cost me."

"Ticket? I don't understand."

"It was a raffle. Each ticket cost two dollars and I bought one ticket and I won. I won the quilt!"

"Well now," she says, pausing. "That is an amazing story, a *most* amazing story. Tell me, how many tickets did the Quilt Circle sell for this raffle?"

"Um, I don't know exactly. They printed off a thousand tickets and my number was 7-7-7, so I figure they sold at least that many."

"At two dollars apiece? Why, I could get five bucks a pop down here—"

The line goes silent, and dead air crackles in my ear. "Mom? Mom, are you still there?"

"Yes, I'm still here...but it's time for me to go. I'm sorry I couldn't send you anything for Christmas. Tell you what. I'll make it up to you soon as I get out, okay? I got a friend that's on top of a sure-fire deal."

Sure-fire deal....

"No, it's okay. I don't need a present—" I hear dead space crackle in my ear again, and then a buzz. "Mom— Mom!" The connection has been broken.

I look at the Huckabys—all six of them. Even the four ninjas have come downstairs for the occasion. "She liked the quilt," I say. "It, uh, it was a real good...remembrance."

"Well," FJ says, looking at Lizzie, "since we're all up, why don't we open presents now and have breakfast later."

"Good idea." Lizzie leads the way to the front room.

I follow behind, but I don't care about presents. I've already had the best present of all. Mom loved my quilt.

8:48 A.M.

"But I thought I was gonna get a cell phone," Matt says, looking at his stash of opened gifts. Mountains of ripped paper and ribbons fill the front room.

"Yeah, and a new electronic game," Mark says.

Luke and Johnny look disappointed, too.

"We talked about this," FJ says, giving them his look. "As soon as things have...settled down, we'll see about those things."

He talked to them without me there? Of course, I think. He was explaining how much extra I'm costing them, which is why they didn't get what they wanted.

Even if it's a skimpy Christmas, all of us—legitimate as well as illegitimate—get new jeans and shirts and socks. Plus board games like IQ and Scrabble to share. I figure they're meant to help us be all that we can be.

Lizzie and FJ really seem to like the scarves that I give them. And Huckaby Numbers Two, Three, Four, and Five wolf down their chocolate-covered pretzels before breakfast.

They didn't give me anything, but I don't care.

Considering I'm the cause of them getting ripped off for Christmas, I don't say anything.

12:55 P.M.

At dinner Lizzie lets me pick my favorite piece of turkey because I'm new. I choose a huge drumstick, and FJ takes the other one. I can almost see smoke coming out of Matt's ears. For the first time since I arrived, I like being number one.

"Just wait till summer gets here," he whispers as we're clearing the table. "I'll show you. I'm gonna leave you in my dust."

"I already told you," I whisper back. "I don't wanna race you."

"Chicken! I'm gonna tell everyone that you're a chicken-livered coward!"

Another nickname. I could hear the taunt that would be thrown at me: Chicken-livered Freaky Sneaky Slow Frankie Joe.

"Well," Matt says. "What'd'ya say? I'm not gonna quit until you race me."

I don't need Huckaby Number Two dogging my every move for the rest of the winter. I need to make up for the money I've spent on presents and postage.

"All right, all right," I mumble. "I'll race you...in April."

Matt looks puzzled. "Why April?"

"Um, because you can't count on the snow being

gone until then." I don't tell him that I plan on being gone before the race. "Better to play it safe. This winter's been a doozy."

Matt blinks. "Guess that makes sense. School will be out for spring break, too. Okay then, second week in April. Deal?"

Second week in April. I like that date. I'll be *long* gone by then.

"Deal," I say, grinning.

Thursday, December 31

4:30 P.M.

I'm watching The Disney Channel with Mark, Luke, and Johnny. Matt is working on a special project in the kitchen.

"I'm thirsty," Johnnie says. "Go get us some more apple juice, Frankie Joe. We're all out."

Lizzie made homemade pretzels and caramel corn to celebrate New Year's Eve. FJ said we could stay up to watch the ball drop in Times Square tonight.

"Why me?"

" 'Cause you're biggest. You can carry heavy stuff."

"I guess that makes sense."

In the kitchen, Lizzie and FJ are sitting at the table with Matt. Lizzie is cutting out paper snowflakes, and FJ is gluing blue crepe paper to a shoe box with a slit in the top. Matt is pasting one of his school pictures to a big poster.

Lizzie smiles at me. "You boys doing okay in there?"

"Yes ma'am. But we're out of juice."

I peek over Matt's shoulder. One of his school pictures is stuck in the middle of a giant snowflake. Smaller snowflakes are glued around the edges. Underneath the picture, he's printed, #1 BEST CHOICE FOR ICE CRYSTAL PRINCE.

"Ice Crystal Prince? What's that?"

"A contest held for fifth-graders," FJ says. "It's a way to break up the long winter. Snowflakes look like ice crystals, which is how the contest got its name." He laughs quietly. "We've got plenty of both this time of year."

"So...it's a popularity contest?"

"Oh, it's more than that," Lizzie says. "It's a way to recognize an outstanding fifth-grade girl and boy. Winners are announced in February. Each fifth-grader is given two ballots—one for a girl and one for a boy—and have this month to vote." She indicates the shoe box that FJ is working on. "Ballot boxes are placed in the school principal's office. Students go there to cast their votes."

She hands me a liter of apple juice. "Matt came up with his own slogan. What do you think?"

I think Matt has number one on the brain, I think, reading his slogan again.

FJ and Lizzie are looking at me. Matt is waiting for my answer, too, his eyes narrow slits.

"I think he's a shoo-in," I say, turning to leave.

"You got that right," Matt says, grinning his cocky grin.

"Well now, I heard Pete Riley is running," Lizzie says. "And Freddy Mendez, too. They're both nice boys."

Matt's face clouds up. "Are you saying I might lose?"

"Your mother's just saying it doesn't pay to count your chickens before they're hatched," FJ says. "You have a month to convince your classmates you're the best candidate."

Lizzie smiles her big smile. "That's right. You just have to make sure your classmates know you're running." Suddenly she looks at me. "You're in the same grade, Frankie Joe. Do you have any ideas?"

Great.

"Um, maybe more posters? The more people that see him, the more votes he'll get. That's what politicians do."

"Your brother's right." Lizzie hands Matt another piece of poster board. "I'll cut out more snowflakes."

Brother? No way!

"I'll help," FJ says, giving me an approving nod.

I leave with the apple juice, listening to the sound of scissors going *snip-snip.*

7:00 P.M.

"Tomato soup and grilled-cheese sandwiches for supper," Lizzie announces." She sets the food on a table. "Show your brothers the posters you made, Matt."

Even though they are all the same, Matt shows us each of the six posters he plans to put up on the first

190

day back at school. The others applaud every time he holds up a new one.

At nine o'clock, the four ninjas and I go upstairs to put on our pajamas and slippers. "To save time later," FJ explains. When we get back downstairs, Lizzie has ice-cream sundaes waiting for us.

Little Johnny falls asleep around ten o'clock, and FJ carries him upstairs.

Just before midnight, Lizzie passes around whistles. We blow them as the ball drops; then Lizzie leads us in the wave. Horns honk up and down the block.

When everyone stops laughing, we carry the dirty dishes to the kitchen sink.

"Go on to bed, boys," FJ says. "Your mom and I will take care of this. And everyone can sleep in late tomorrow morning."

It's been a nice New Year's, I decide as I walk upstairs. But as I crawl into bed, I think of Mom and feel sad. She loved New Year's Eve. I wonder if she got to watch the ball drop this year...or if the prison guards turned off the lights.

Monday, January 4

7:45 A.M.

The soybean green walls at school are covered with paper snowflakes and candidate posters. Mandy is running for Ice Crystal Princess. I smile as I look at her poster, which reads GOOD THINGS COME IN LITTLE PACKAGES.

Matt left early for school so he could tape his posters to the walls. Wherever I turn, I run into a smiling Matt Huckaby. Instead of being Mr. Show-off in class, now he's Mr. Nice Guy: volunteering to tutor kids who need help, running errands for the teachers. He's working overtime to make sure he gets recognized.

In last period, we're all given two paper snowflakes: one for Ice Crystal Prince and one for Ice Crystal Princess. I stuff mine inside my backpack. I don't care who wins.

3:48 P.M.

The Great Escape is busting with kids. Because it's bitterly cold outside, more parents have put their children into the program. Mrs. Bixby has to work double hard to watch everyone. Even so, she can't keep up.

"*Ow*," Mandy yells as a book bounces off the back of her head. "This is ridiculous, Mrs. Bixby. I can't finish my homework with kids throwing stuff and yelling. You need an assistant."

"I've already checked, Mandy. There's no money to hire one."

A pencil flies past my nose. "Hey," I say to the kindergartner that threw it. "Cut it out."

"Who did that?" Mrs. Bixby says, looking around. "You could put an eye out."

The kid who threw the pencil gives me a please-don't-snitch look. "Not sure," I say. The boy telegraphs *thank you* with his eyes, then lowers his head over his book.

"I got it!" Mandy says to Mrs. Bixby. "You could use students. Those of us in fifth grade could be your helpers."

"Can't break the rules," she says. "Everyone must practice their spelling and math; then do their homework." She shakes her head as she looks around the hectic room. "Besides, the other kids wouldn't do what you tell them. They only listen to grown-ups."

Right. Like they're listening to you.

4:15 P.M.

The noise is deafening. Kids are yelling to go to the restroom. Others howl for games and coloring books.

Some complain because it's past snack time and they're hungry. The first-grade table starts throwing crayons at the kindergartners. I have a mountain of homework, and I feel like there's a hundred coyotes howling at me.

"There's no way we can study!" I yell, jumping to my feet. "You gotta give Mandy's idea a try!"

Mrs. Bixby comes to a stop in the middle of the room. All the kids freeze in place. The quiet is extraordinarily loud.

"It's just"—I look at the faces around the fifth-grade table—"I don't want to haul all these books home through the snow. Do you?"

"Yeah," Mandy says. "We're never gonna get our homework done if you don't let us help, Mrs. Bixby. You can be the boss; we'll do other things. Like hand out snacks. Or take the little ones to the restroom. And Frankie Joe's as tall as you are, so he can reach the games at the top of the storage cabinet."

"He's older than everyone else, too," Luke yells. "He's almost a grown-up."

"Yeah, and he's a good tiebreaker!" Little Johnny says from across the room. "He's the tiebreaker in our house. He's a real good tiebreaker."

"And fast," Mark says from the fourth-grade table, "because his legs are so long."

"Let Frankie Joe be in charge," Mandy says, grinning at me. "He can delegate to the rest of us."

"But I'm Student Council representative," Matt protests. "I should be in charge—"

"Oh shut up, Matt," Mandy says.

"Vote! Vote!" kids begin to yell. "All for Frankie Joe?" Hands shoot into the air.

At that moment, Principal Arnt walks into the room. His mouth falls open as he takes in the bedlam. "What's going on here? I can hear the commotion clear down at my office."

Mrs. Bixby's mouth thaws out so she can talk again. "Why, we're just reorganizing, Mr. Arnt. You see, I've just appointed a student to help me out. Frankie Joe Huckaby's going to organize the fifth grade to assist with snacks and games and restroom duty. That way I can handle study assignments." She pauses to catch her breath. "And we did it the democratic way, with an election. That's what the noise was all about."

"Oh," Mr. Arnt says. "Well now, that sounds like a good idea." As he turns to leave the room, he stops and looks at Mrs. Bixby again. "Did you say *Frankie Joe Huckaby*?"

"Yes, that's exactly what I said."

Quickly she turns to me. "Well don't just stand there, Frankie Joe," she whispers. "Start delegating!"

"Mandy, you're in charge of snacks! Um, you two, line up those who need to go to the restrooms—one line for girls, one for boys! The rest of you, pick up crayons and erasers!" I take down a handful of games from the storage cabinet and hand them to Matt. Looking dazed he passes them out to waiting kids.

As Mr. Arnt leaves the room, Mrs. Bixby remains frozen to the floor, a look of shock on her face. "Why it's working," she mumbles. "It's actually working."

The only one in the room more dumbfounded than Mrs. Bixby is me.

Suddenly Mrs. Bixby smiles at me. "I'm proud of the way you took charge, Frankie Joe. *Very* proud."

"Thanks."

Mom would be proud of me, too, I think. I can hardly wait to tell her.

I like being in charge. It makes me feel...taller.

Saturday, January 9

10:30 A.M.

"Where you goin', Oddball?" Mandy waves me down.

"Oh, hey Mandy." I pull over to the curb where she's standing outside the town's café. "I'm making deliveries for Miss Peachcott. What's up?"

"You wanna get a hot chocolate? I been meaning to talk to you about something."

Hot chocolate! I'd love a hot chocolate, but that would mean spending some of my stash.

"My treat," Mandy says, reading my mind. "It's important."

Parking my bike, I follow her inside. We kick the slush off our boots, unzip parkas and pull off mittens, then slide into a booth. When the waitress walks up, Mandy orders two hot cocoas and an order of cheesy fries.

"So what's so important? I got other business with Miss Peachcott today." I don't tell Mandy about my job as tester and dabber. I'm tired of livening things up in this one-horse town.

"I wanna talk about business, too," she says. "*School* business. I've decided you should run for Ice Crystal Prince."

"What? I don't care anything about that."

"But you gotta care. You'll be running against Matt."

"Running against Matt! Are you crazy?"

"I already told him that you were going to. He was mad enough to bite nails in half."

"You what? Why'd you go and do that?"

"Why not?"

" 'Cause I'm not gonna do it."

The waitress brings our order, and we sit still until she leaves, glaring at each other.

"Why not?" Mandy asks again when we're alone. "You gotta be tired of him rubbing your nose in it all the time. I know *I'm* tired of it."

"I wouldn't stand a chance." I stuff my mouth full of fries, wondering what Mandy would do if I told her the truth. I decide I can't risk it, not this close to leaving Clearview in my dust.

"Sure you would," she says. "The fifth-graders in The Great Escape respect you now that you're Mrs. Bixby's assistant. I know I could get them to support you—and talk to their friends. Someone needs to put Matt in his place."

She's right. Someone does need to give Matt his

comeuppance, but that someone's not me. I have other things on my mind. My escape.

"I can't," I say. Slurping down my cocoa, I get up to leave.

"Wait," she says. "Why not?"

"I . . . I just can't, that's all."

Mandy grabs my arm. "I been a good friend, Frankie Joe Huckaby. You owe me a reason—a *real* reason."

She has been a good friend. One of the best.

" 'Cause . . . 'cause he's my brother."

"I can't believe you said that," she snorts. "It doesn't seem to make any difference with him."

I know, I think as I zip up my parka. But she didn't see how hard Lizzie and FJ worked on Matt's posters and ballot box. And she didn't see how important it was for Matt to be number one again at something.

"You're weird, Frankie Joe Huckaby," she yells at me. "*Weird* Scared Sneaky Freaky Slow Frankie Joe!"

Great. Now my only friend is calling me names.

1:15 P.M.

Matt ambushes me as soon as I get back from Miss Peachcott's house.

"You're running against me!" He shoves my bike and me down in a snowbank. "I hate you, Frankie Joe. You've messed up everything since you came here. I wish you'd get run over by a snowplow . . . or freeze to death in a blizzard."

Tears are sliding down his cheeks, and his nose is running. I figure out he's talking about the Ice Crystal Contest. "Hey, I'm not—"

"Mandy told me. You're gonna split the vote so I won't win Ice Crystal Prince. You know the kids in The Great Escape will vote for you."

"Matt—I'm not running!"

He wipes his nose on his sleeve. "You're...not?"

"No." I get up out of the snowbank and brush off my clothes. "That was Mandy's idea. I told her this morning I'm not gonna do it."

"But...why?"

Why do people always want a reason?

" 'Cause"—I try to think of a lie—" 'cause FJ would say it wasn't right." Which is the truth.

"Yeah," he mumbles. "Yeah, he wouldn't like us running against each other."

"And it would hurt Lizzie. *She's* been nice to me since I came here."

Matt's face turns red.

"It's no big deal to me." Which is the truth. It's a huge deal to Matt, but all I care about is getting back home.

"Sorry about your bike." Matt picks up my bike and pushes it to the front porch. "And, uh, I didn't mean those things I said. I was just mad. Okay?"

"It's okay," I tell him. "I've wished those same things about you. I guess I didn't mean them, either."

"You *guess*?"

I just grin.

9:36 P.M.

That night I rewrite my escape plan after I've finished my chores and homework.

Tarp Found one half price at the farm supply store.

Spare bike tube and flat kit Bought at the gas station.

Pot for cooking Salvaged.

Matches to start a fire Picked up three books at Gambino's Pizza Parlor.

Canteen Have two empty plastic bottles.

Jacket My Michelin-Man jacket.

Bungee cord The one Lizzie gave me for pizza delivery.

Money Still need more.

Mementos Need plastic bags to keep them dry and clean. Get from the kitchen.

Triple A maps Need a plastic bag for them, too.

Clothes All set.

"Now all I have to do is wait for the snow to melt—"

I hear a creak on the stairs and see FJ come into view. Hurriedly I close my notebook.

He walks over to me. "What's this I'm hearing?"

I wonder if Matt squealed about me looking for the tarp? Or if Mr. Puffin told him I was asking questions about when the snow ended?

"Mr. Arnt told me that you were elected Mrs. Bixby's assistant."

"Oh," I say, feeling relieved. "It wasn't my idea."

"Well, I hear it was you stepped up to fix the problem. Glad to see you've learned what that means." He points to the definition of responsibility taped to the wall.

He thinks *that's* why I did it?

He checks his watch. "Almost time for lights-out. Just wanted to tell you to keep up the good work."

"Thanks," I mumble.

FJ hesitates at the top of the stairs, a serious look on his face. "Growing up means you accept responsibility, even when it's not easy. Sometimes that involves difficult decisions." He looks at me. "You understand what I'm telling you, Frankie Joe?"

I look at the definition on the wall again. "Um, I think so."

"Good. Lights-out in five minutes." The stairs creak again as he goes downstairs.

I remove the definition for *responsibility* from the wall and throw it into the wastebasket.

Woo-hoo. He's telling me I don't have to read this definition anymore.

Saturday, January 16

9:30 A.M.

Everything's a frozen desert when I bike to Miss Peach-cott's house. Dunes of snow are everywhere. But I don't feel the cold because Miss Peachcott has taken on a new customer, and that means I have an extra delivery.

"Come in, Frankie Joe," Miss Peachcott says. "Have a cookie while I finish up this order."

More Girl Scout cookies. Peanut butter this time.

"That divorcée Miz Bloom asked me to fix this up for her." She screws the cap down on a jar of cream she's concocted. "I have helped many a woman beat dry, chapped skin, but this one's been a real challenge." She pauses. "Could be that job she's got. Waitressing is hard on a person."

Yeah. Mom hated her waitress job. If this new deal with her friend works out, maybe she won't have to do it anymore. I don't care what she does as long as we're back together again.

"You got any new blemish concoctions to try before I go?" I ask.

"Check back with me later. I was up most of the night working on this dry-skin formula. My customers must come first." She hands me a Nova bag. "Get goin' now. Miz Bloom sounded desperate."

9:55 A.M.

My Rover Sport's tires cause the slush on the salted roads to spray like waves. February days are growing longer and that makes me happy. Soon March will be here, and the snow will be gone. Just like me.

"Hey, Frankie Joe," Ms. Bloom says when I knock on her door. "Come on in. I need to write out a check."

I set the Nova bag on her coffee table. "Uh, Miss Peachcott mixed this up special," I say to fill the time as she hunts for her checkbook.

"I hope it works," she says, sighing. "I look like I've been down one too many rough roads." She glances at me, smiling. "Well, maybe I have. I guess you've heard that I hold the record for number of marriages in this town—and divorces."

I shrug. "I guess you've heard about me, too."

She lets out a little laugh. "People in small towns look hard for ways to liven things up." She opens the jar of cream I brought. "I figure the dishwater at the café and this cold weather are why my skin feels like grit.

It's as dried out and rough as sandpaper and"—she rubs some cream on her face—"tough as boot leather."

Just like Mr. O'Hare's, I think. And mine.

I take a special liking for Ms. Bloom and her face that's been down too many rough roads. I've ridden down some bad ones myself this winter, and the cold wind has blistered my face, too.

"You think this new cream Elsie made for me will help?" she asks.

"Yes ma'am, I do."

I hope that's not a lie.

Friday, January 22

6:45 P.M.

"You're uncommonly quiet, Liz," FJ says, pouring himself a cup of coffee. He sits down at the table across from Lizzie.

I notice that Lizzie is staring into space. It's after supper, and it's my turn to stack the dishwasher. We had sloppy joes on hamburger buns with potato chips and coleslaw, so clean up is easy. The half brothers have gone to the living room to watch TV.

"It's just"—she lowers her voice—"I heard the Ice Princess race is a runaway. One candidate is getting most of the votes."

My ears perk up. That has to be Mandy. She's an A-plus salesperson.

"But the race for Prince is close."

Woo-hoo! Matt might lose the contest.

"Where'd you hear that?" FJ pours milk in his coffee.

"From a couple of people at the school. Mr. Arnt's secretary keeps track of ballots, counts them daily."

Lizzie glances at me, and lowers her voice some more. "What if Matt *doesn't* win? I don't know what to do."

FJ looks at me. "Finish up there, Frankie Joe, and join your brothers in the front room."

"Yes sir, just got the last dish in."

I pause outside the kitchen door, listening.

"It would break Matt's heart," I hear Lizzie say. "He's known his classmates all his life."

"Some things are out of our hands, Liz. He doesn't win, well...he doesn't win. He'll hold up. He's a Huckaby."

"But I just don't want him hurt. I don't want any of them to get hurt."

"Can't hold them in your apron strings forever."

"I know...I know."

"Trust me. Our boys might bend in a storm, but they won't break."

In the living room, I sit on the opposite end of the sofa from Matt. A movie is showing, but I can't concentrate on it. I hear Mark and Luke laugh now and then, and Little Johnny squeal. I keep glancing at Matt, but it's like he's wearing a mask. One that doesn't smile or frown.

Friday, January 29

3:20 P.M.

Math class, my last period. I hand in my assignment, pull out my backpack, and wait for the final bell. Suddenly the PA system squeals, and we're listening to Mr. Arnt's voice.

"This announcement is for fifth-graders. Today is the deadline for casting your votes in the Ice Crystal Contest. So those of you who haven't turned in your ballots yet, drop them off at my office right after school." He pauses. "Voting is a privilege, not something to be taken frivolously. The candidates have worked hard to earn your vote. Don't let them down."

Another squeal, and it's quiet again. I remember the two ballots I stuffed into my backpack and look for them. They're still there. Lying at the bottom, wrinkled and bent.

I pull them out. One has a girl's head on it and the words *Ice Crystal Princess* printed underneath. I catch Mandy's eye, hold up the girl's ballot, and smile, letting her know I plan to vote for her. She rolls her eyes at me.

Ouch. I feel my smile turn upside down.

I glance at Matt. He's looking right at me—and at the boy's ballot in my hand. I watch as he begins to chew on his bottom lip and blink a lot. He wants that vote in his box.

When the bell rings, Matt is the first one out the door.

On the way to the after-school program, I go by Mr. Arnt's office. Mandy's ballot box is easy to spot. It's covered in white crepe paper and has pink snowflakes all over it. I know she doesn't need my vote, but I feel good as I stuff my ballot into the slit on the top.

Because I watched FJ and Lizzie work on Matt's box, I recognize his box, too. I pull the wrinkled ballot for Ice Crystal Prince out of my backpack and stuff it into his box.

As I turn to leave, I see Matt standing in the doorway with Mr. Arnt. He's holding some papers, and I figure out he's been talking Student Council business.

"Good job, Frankie Joe," Mr. Arnt says, nodding at me. He looks at Matt. "One of your constituents just voted for you. Don't you have something to say?"

Matt squeezes, "Thanks," out of his mouth.

Payback feels really good.

"You boys better get going. Don't want Mrs. Bixby wondering where you are."

Matt and I walk down the hall together, not talking and not looking at each other.

"You still may not win," I whisper as we walk into the room.

"I know," he says, sitting down across from me.

"But if you don't, it won't be my fault."

If Matt doesn't win, he can't blame anyone but himself.

Saturday, January 30

9:15 P.M.

It's almost bedtime, and I take out my escape plan. I glance at the calendar on the wall to check the date.

Going over my escape list now, I add a new item.

W-D 40 The garage in town will have some.

I hear a *creak* on the stairs. Closing my notebook, I turn to see if it's one of the ninjas. But it's FJ, and he has a serious look on his face.

"I do something wrong?"

He sits down on the edge of my desk and pulls a piece of paper from his shirt pocket. "Matter of fact, you've done something right—very right. Take a look at your latest report card."

On the left-hand side is a list of subjects: English, Math, Science, History. Each quarter's grades are shown in columns to the right, next to the subjects. In the first quarter the letters in the grade column had been Ds and even a couple of Fs. In the next one, I see one C, two Bs, and an A.

I feel my mouth drop open. I knew my grades had been getting better. The teachers had been writing things like "excellent" and "good work" on my papers. But I never expected this.

"An A," I say. "I got an A in Math!"

FJ smiles. "So you see, things are going very right. Don't you agree?"

"Yes sir!"

I watch his mouth go straight again. There's something else....

"You've, uh, you've done well since you came here to live, Frankie Joe," he says, "real well. Studied hard, worked hard...very, very well."

Why is he repeating himself?

"Yes indeed," he continues. "In the last few months, you done *exceptionally* well." FJ begins wiping at his mouth like something sticky is stuck on it. "And we're thinking—Lizzie and me—that as long as you're here, you will continue to do well."

What's he saying?

"So that's why we began legal procedures sometime back. I'm going to be sole custodian for you—that means your legal guardian—and Lizzie is going to adopt you. It normally takes four to six months, so it should be final in another few weeks."

Four to six months? I remember hearing FJ and

Lizzie saying those words once before. They were talking in the kitchen when I snuck downstairs to look for matches for my escape. They were talking about me!

"No," I say. "No no no! I got to go back to Laredo and live with Mom."

FJ's mouth is thin as a pencil line. "Your mama needs some time to get back on her feet, son. That might take a good bit of time. She can visit you any time she wants; I'll see to that—"

"She won't let it happen! She won't let you do this!"

FJ hesitates. "I've, uh, I've discussed this with Martha Jane. She knows we've filed the papers."

"She...*what?*" My chest feels like it's caving in. Why didn't she say something to me?

"Lizzie wanted me to say something earlier," he says, "but I've waited until I could show you that you'd be better off here. Look at your school records." He points to the report card. "Doesn't that say it all? And the best news is that Mr. Arnt and I have been talking about allowing you to skip a grade—just like Mark did. If you go to summer school and continue to work hard, you can move up to the seventh grade next year where you belong."

That was the reason for the school visits?

"Surely you can see it's best for you to stay here?"

Here again. *Here* in Clearview, Illinois. A million miles from Laredo, Texas.

I throw the grade report in the wastebasket. "No sir, that doesn't say it all. *I* say it all—and I don't want to get adopted and stay here. I wanna go back home to Laredo."

FJ stands up and pulls the grade report out of the trash. "It's all but a done deal, Frankie Joe. All that's left is for Martha Jane to sign the papers...and I know she will. There's not a court in the land that would give her custody now, not with her record." He holds up my report card. "Especially with how well you're doing here."

He lays his hand on my shoulder. "Why, people in this town think the world of you—we all do." He pauses. "Especially me. I want you here with me, Frankie Joe. I want to be a good father to you, make up for all those years we lost."

I stare at FJ, realizing how much I've wanted to hear those words all the months I sat in the attic doing homework. But now all I want to do is cry.

Sometimes words just come too late.

9:45 P.M.

Dear Mom,

FJ told me tonight about becoming my sole custodian and Lizzie adopting me. I told him you wouldn't let that happen. You got to talk to your lawyer about stopping them. I want to come home to live with you.

Please hurry.

Frankie Joe

XOXOXO

Saturday, February 13

9:00 A.M.

Matt's trophy sits in the middle of the kitchen table. It's a bronze snowflake with a plate at the bottom that reads SNOW CRYSTAL PRINCE. He won by three votes, but the way he's grinning, you'd think it was three hundred.

As she hands Matt some waffles, Lizzie says, "Your brother's idea to make extra posters probably made the difference, don't you think?"

"Yeah." Matt gives me a look. "That's probably it."

We've never mentioned Mandy's idea that I run against him.

Mandy won, too—by a landslide. She didn't need my vote, but I'm glad I voted anyway. Maybe I'll write to her when I get back to Texas and tell her I voted for her. I wonder if she would write back. Or if she doesn't believe in writing, either...like Mom.

Why haven't I heard from Mom?

10:15 A.M.

Miss Peachcott shows me the rash on her neck and face. "The doctor says it's shingles."

"What causes it?"

"Chicken pox."

I take a step back. I don't want to catch chicken pox. Chicken pox would interfere with my delivery service. And anything that interferes with my delivery service would stop me from leaving. Though I haven't heard from Mom yet, I'm sure she's got her lawyer working on it.

"Oh, no need to worry," she says. "It's not the catching kind. It affects the nerves. Doctor told me I've been carrying this virus since I had the chicken pox as a girl. It's just come back, that's all."

"Why did it come back?"

"Doctor didn't know why, but I do. It's because I have to get this formula right for my blemish concealer. That's why the chicken pox has come back now— because I'm a case of nerves!" She sits down at the table, looking sad. "And to top it off, the doctor told me I cannot put anything on my hair or face. You know what that means?"

I notice that Miss Peachcott's hair has been cut short and is mostly white now. Snow white and fluffy as a snowflake. And her skin is pink as a Nova bag. Except her birthmark, which looks like nothing more than a giant brown freckle.

I suck the spit from between my teeth. "Yes ma'am," I say. "It means now you look pretty."

Her eyes go round as pie plates. "Why, how can you make fun of me at a time like this?"

"I'm not making fun of you, Miss Peachcott. Look at yourself in the mirror. Except for where the shingles show. Don't look at that."

She does look in the mirror, but her eyes go straight to the shingles. She plops the mirror on the table. "It's all I can see—that rash."

I think a bit, then pick up the mirror again. "Okay, so look at the rash."

"What? Why would I want to look at that?"

"Just look at it."

She picks up the mirror again. At first her eyes bobble, but then she holds them steady.

"Do you see the birthmark when you're looking at the rash?"

"Why no," she says. "All I see is the—"

She lays the mirror down and sits quiet for a time. I begin to squirm, wondering if I've lost another friend. I reach for my parka, getting ready to leave, but Miss Peachcott lays her hand on my arm.

"So what you're telling me is, a person sees what they want to see. That right, Frankie Joe Huckaby?"

"Yes ma'am, I guess that's what I'm saying. That and...well, I don't like you any less because you've got a birthmark, and I bet no one else does, either. Your customers come to you 'cause they know you'll help them. Like Miz Bloom, who doesn't want leathery skin. And Mrs. Wilkins who needs something for her chapped hands. And—"

"That sweet little newlywed, Mrs. Barnes," Miss Peachcott interrupts. "Who doesn't want to smell like baby burp."

"Yeah, and..." I blow the air from my lungs.

"Well, spit it out," she says. "You know how I feel about people that diddle-dawdle with their words."

"Well," I say, pulling a deep breath, "when you put your newest concoction on the birthmark, that's *all* I see." I wave my hands around the kitchen at jars and tubes of concealer she's concocted. All failures. "It's like all this is a rainbow, and you're looking for—"

"The pot of gold at the end of it," she says, interrupting me again. She pauses. "I was hoping to sell my formula so I could retire, live the good life. If I quit now, I'll have to keep on working."

Quit! She can't quit. Neither of us are quitters.

"Wait," I say. "What would you do if you did retire, Miss Peachcott?"

"What?"

"I mean, is it because you want to leave this one-horse town in the dust?"

Like I do?

She looks startled. "Why no, Clearview's my home. I'd never leave Clearview."

"Oh. Well then, do you want to travel? Is that why you need the money, so you can see other places? Is that the good life you're talking about?"

"Heavens no, I don't like to fly. I get airsick—and it's not safe anymore. All that violence out there..." She waves a hand toward the TV. "Watching the Travel Channel is better than flying hours and hours, especially now you have to take off your shoes and go through those machines and get patted down like a criminal."

She looks around her kitchen laboratory. "It's just that, without my formula, there's...nothing."

"You can still sell Nova."

"Oh, anyone can sell Nova! It's just that"—she waves her arm at the dozens and dozens of pink paper bags—"none of it is *my* creation."

A lightbulb goes on. "Work on your other formula, then—the one you made for Miz Bloom. There's plenty of people here that need help with rough skin. These Alberta clippers suck the moisture out of people like a sponge."

"What?" She sits quiet, considering this. "Why, of course. An emollient tailored exclusively for Clearview. The one I made for Miz Bloom is working better than what Nova sells—and I bet I can make it even better!"

"E–molly–*what*?"

"E–mol–li–ent. It's a remedy for skin problems. Why I could use Miz Bloom as my test subject."

She grows quiet again, so quiet I begin to squirm. "You want me to leave?"

All at once, she comes alive. "Well, of course I want you to leave! We must take care of our customers. They're depending on us."

Her eyes light up like a fire is heating them. "You know, Mrs. Barnes needs an air freshener in the worst way. She had her baby girls into the doctor's office for colic while I was there. Their milk is souring their stomachs, you see—makes them spit up; it smells bad. Maybe I'll just create a new air freshener, too."

"Lilac," I say, grinning. "Lilacs cover the smell of most anything. That's why farmers plant them around their cow pastures."

She smiles. "Lilac it is."

11:35 A.M.

Dear Mom,

I haven't heard from you about the lawyer yet. Please let me know what is happening. FJ reads your letters, so maybe you can call me. Let me know when your lawyer is finished talking with his lawyer about stopping things. Hurry!!!!

Frankie Joe
XOXOXO

I quickly put the letter into an envelope and put a stamp on it. The post office closes at noon on Saturdays now that Christmas is over, and I want to get this to Mom right away.

"Another letter?" the postmaster asks when I walk in.

"Yes ma'am. Can you still get it on the truck?"

"Consider it gone," she says, smiling.

12:20 P.M.

The man at the garage asks, "Can I help you find something, Frankie Joe?"

"No sir, I just found it." I set a can of WD-40 on the counter and pull out enough money to pay for it.

"Thanks."

It's the last thing I need to buy for my escape.

9:10 P.M.

Just before lights-out, I look up *emollient* in my dictionary. Definitions are tricky. Sometimes there's more than one for a word. I read through them all until I find the one that I like best for Ms. Bloom.

emol·lient \ *adj*: making less intense or harsh.

I climb into bed feeling good because of my talk with Miss Peachcott. Now I can skip town without feeling like I deserted her. And I'm positive that her shingles rash will clear up as soon as she gets her case of nerves under control.

Mr. Puffin and my other customers will be fine, too. Someone else will take up my delivery business. Maybe Mandy. She's a natural at business. I grin, picturing short Mandy on her short bike delivering pizzas to Mr. Puffin and Mr. Lindholm.

Mrs. Bixby will find someone else to be her assistant in the after-school program, too. Some of the fourth-graders have shot up this year—almost as tall as me.

And Matt will be in hog heaven because he'll be the number-one Huckaby again. With me gone, he can get a cell phone . . . and the others can get the new electronic games and other things they didn't get for Christmas. And Lizzie and FJ won't have to buy me any more clothes at a fifteen-percent discount. Or pay for me to go to The Great Escape. They'll save money on food, too, and won't have to open another Christmas Club account.

Everyone will be better off when I'm gone. Everyone.

Saturday, February 27

3:15 P.M.

Thunder in February? Billowing black clouds on the horizon throw lightning bolts at the ground like an alien spaceship attacking the planet. I decide to cancel my test run to Mr. Puffin's farm to check the roads to see if they're free of snowdrifts. Turning around I pedal hard. The wind rattles and shakes my Rover Sport all the way back to Clearview.

I reach the house just as icy rain begins to pelt the slushy streets and pound the porch and bounce off the roof. I hurry upstairs, wondering if I should add a rain slicker to my list. I remember seeing one colored like camouflage in the hunting section of the hardware store—

"What are you doing here?"

Matt's sitting in my desk chair looking at me, eyes round. Glancing around the room, I see my escape plan in his hands... my supplies scattered across the floor... my money stash lying on the desktop.

"I was gonna borrow your History book, and then I got to looking around and...." Matt stares at me, a confused look on his face. "You're...you're running away?"

I reach him in two steps. Grabbing his shirt collar in my hands, I throw him on the floor. The next thing I know, I'm straddling him. "You had no right!" I feel my fist connect with his nose.

"Get off me! Get off!" Matt twists away from me. "But—but I thought you wanted to take my place." His nose is bleeding. "You really want to leave?"

"You had no right." I begin gathering up my things. "Get out."

"It's a stupid idea. It'll never work."

"Yes it will. I made a plan." I wave my notebook in front of his battered nose.

"They'll find you. They'll hunt until they find you."

"I got that figured out, too." I sit down on the bed, feeling really tired.

Matt plops down in my desk chair, dabbing at his nose with a tissue from the box on my desk. "So that's why you wanted that tarp, isn't it? You've been planning this ever since you got here."

"Yeah, stupid. That's why I wanted the tarp."

Matt looks bewildered. "But that means you don't want to be adopted."

"Right again! Would you want to go somewhere hundreds of miles from home to live with strangers—especially if they called you Sneaky Freaky Slow

224

Matt Huckaby? And you were made to look stupid in school—on purpose? And your shorts got soaked in the toilet because you finally got to take a hot shower? I hate it here!"

Matt squirms, looking uncomfortable. "I have to tell Dad."

"Would you get over being stupid? All this time, you've hated me 'cause you thought I wanted to be number one. I don't want to be number one. Once I'm gone, you'll be number one forever."

"But this is dumb—dangerous dumb. I'll...I'll be responsible if I don't tell and you get hurt."

I walk over to him, put my fist in his face. "You owe me. Remember the contest?"

"Yeah...yeah, I know." He still looks dazed. "So when were you planning on leaving?"

"You gonna tell?"

"No, I won't tell. I still think it's dumb, but I'll keep your secret. And we Huckabys keep our word."

"The week before spring break. That's when I'm leaving."

"What? But...but the bike race is the next week. I've told everyone about that race. I was gonna clean your clock, sweep you under the carpet."

"Yeah, well now you don't have to. I'll be gone, and you can go back to being number one—at everything."

"That's not fair." His eyes turn fiery. "The kids would always wonder if you could've beaten me."

"Hey look, that's when I'm leaving."

"Then we'll move the date up." Matt faces me. "You don't race me, I'll tell."

"Okay then, we'll move the date up. Right before I leave town, okay?"

I hold out my hand to shake on the deal. Matt takes it reluctantly.

After Matt leaves, I put my things away and lie down on the bed. I listen to the rain pound the house, the house answer with groans and creeks, and let out my breath. I'm down to counting days now. Days until I'll be riding past cornfields, smelling sun and rain and freedom. Nothing stands in my way. Nothing.

Saturday, March 13

3:15 P.M.

"I'm just gonna take a test drive," I tell Matt as I slip into my backpack. I've loaded it with four of my schoolbooks to get a feel for the load I'll be carrying.

"Want me to come with you?" He's been working on his bike, which he hauled out of the storage shed this morning. "In case you run into trouble?"

"That's the whole idea of doing a test run," I say. "Where'd you leave your smarts, Mr. Honor Student?"

"Oh, right." He grins at me.

I wheel my Rover Sport away from the curb. It's still cool, but the snow is melting fast. As soon as I'm out of town, I begin to pedal faster, and soon I'm cruising past big brown squares of ground waiting to be planted. In the stillness, the same questions that have been bugging me for days pop into my head.

Why hasn't Mom called me? Will she call FJ instead? Or have her lawyer call FJ's lawyer?

"Frankie Joe! Hey, Frankie Joe!"

Looking over my shoulder, I see Matt behind me, pumping hard. I pull to a stop and wait for him to catch up. "What is it?"

"You're supposed to come home. Dad needs to talk to you—right away."

FJ has heard from Mom—the adoption is off! Wheeling around I head back toward town.

"Wait up," Matt calls out. "I need to tell you something else."

I wait for him to catch up. "You didn't tell FJ about my escape plan, did you? You promised you wouldn't tell."

He shakes his head. "I don't break my word. When I make a promise, I keep it."

"Then, what?" We start pedaling again, side by side.

"I'm, uh, I'm gonna call off the race."

"What? But, why?"

"I couldn't catch you, Frankie Joe. I pumped the whole way, and I couldn't catch you." He shakes his head. "You know what that means?"

I don't.

"It means you're faster than me. I figure it's because of your delivery service, all that biking you did this winter."

"Well then," I say, "we'll have the race, and I'll let you beat me. You'll be number one again."

"Why would you do that? Why would you let me win?"

"Won't matter to me 'cause I'll be leaving right after the race. Who cares?"

"You can't let me win. That's not fair. You forget what Dad's always telling us about being all we can be?"

We park our bikes on the front porch. "I'm not sure being all you can be always means being number one, Matt. Know what I mean?"

He shakes his head a little and says, "Hey, I'm supposed to be the smart one. Remember?"

I just grin.

3:47 P.M.

FJ hands me two letters the minute I walk in the front door. They're the ones I sent to Mom.

"But I don't understand."

"They were returned." He looks at Matt. "Your mom's in the kitchen and your brothers are upstairs. Why don't you give Frankie Joe and me some time alone."

"Sure," Matt says. "I'll, uh, I'll take your backpack upstairs, Frankie Joe."

As Matt leaves, I look at the letters. They're both still sealed, so I know FJ hasn't read them. Something has been stamped on the front of them: RETURN TO SENDER. ADDRESSEE NO LONGER AN INMATE.

"What does that mean?" I ask, looking at FJ.

"Your mom's in town, Frankie Joe. She got out of jail early."

"I knew it!" I blurt out. "I knew she wouldn't let me get adopted! She's come to get me, hasn't she?"

"Come on," he says, hurrying me toward the door. "I'll explain at the attorney's office. She's waiting for us there. We don't have a lot of time. She wants to see you before she and Ricky leave."

What?

4:15 P.M.

"M-mom?" I whisper. My tongue feels numb. I feel numb all over.

She looks the same, except her blonde hair is longer and her skin isn't tanned—and she's sitting next to a dark-haired man I don't know. When she sees me, she jumps out of her chair and runs over to me.

"Hi kiddo! Guess you're surprised to see me, huh?" She pulls me close, then pushes me back and gives me an up-and-down look. "Looks like you haven't missed any meals."

"But how'd you get here?...Why didn't you call?... I don't understand."

"Oh things just got moving too fast," she says, brushing her hand through the air. "And you're the one got me here—got *us* here."

She nods toward the man sitting at the table. "This is Ricky. Remember, I told you about him. Would you believe I raffled off that quilt you sent and got a bundle for it—enough to pay our way here. And FJ's staking me to a new start—*us* a new start." Again she looks at the dark-haired man.

What?

"Martha Jane," FJ says, frowning. "I didn't have time to explain things to Frankie Joe—"

"You were right, FJ," she interrupts. "He is doing better up here than he would do tagging along after me."

What? It's like my ears can't keep up with her mouth.

The man named Ricky walks over to me. "Don't worry, kid, I'll take good care of her." He looks at his watch, then at Mom.

"Okay," she tells him, then looks at me again. "Time to hit the road, hon." She kisses me quick on the forehead. "Now do what FJ tells you. He showed me your report card. I'm real proud of you."

The man named Ricky takes her arm, and she says okay again.

"I really gotta go," she tells me. "We got a lot of ground to cover. Ricky got us both jobs in Reno. I'll send you my address soon as we get settled. Keep those letters coming."

"No—wait!" I grab her arm. "What about our trailer in Laredo? Mr. Lopez and Mr. O'Hare fixed the front steps."

"Trailer? Oh, I guess I forgot to tell you. The bank took it back for nonpayment." As the door closes behind her I hear her say, "There's nothing there for either of us to go back to."

6:05 P.M.

FJ drives quietly for several minutes. "I'm real sorry, Frankie Joe. I didn't know she was coming, either. She just showed up and"—he goes quiet again—"she, uh, she wanted a stake and wouldn't sign the papers until..." He sighs. "One day you'll see it was the right thing to do."

I go straight upstairs when we reach the house. Rushing to my desk, I rip my escape plan out of my notebook and tear it to shreds.

Sunday, March 14

8:15 A.M.

"I fixed a surprise for breakfast," Lizzie says, opening the curtains to let light into the room. "Just for you. Breakfast burritos."

I pull the quilt over my head.

"Come on, Frankie Joe," FJ says. "The boys are waiting for us."

"I'm not hungry," I say through the quilt. I hear FJ sigh.

"He just needs time, Frank," Lizzie whispers. "Let's give him some time."

Creaking stairs tell me they're gone. I slip out of bed and pull the curtains closed again.

12:30 P.M.

"Dad sent us up to get you," Little Johnny says. "You have to come down to eat." Luke and Mark are standing behind him.

"Go away," I say.

"But—"

"Tell them I'm not hungry."

"But you gotta be hungry—"

"Just leave!" I pull the quilt over my head.

5:20 P.M.

FJ sticks a thermometer into my mouth. "Make sure you hold it under your tongue."

"Could be he's caught something," Lizzie says. "He's been working awfully hard, and this winter's been a bad one. Might be the flu. There's a new virus going around, too."

FJ sighs as he reads the thermometer. "Ninety-eight point six. His temperature's normal."

I crawl back under the covers.

Monday, March 15

7:25 A.M.

"Come on, Frankie Joe," Matt says. "We got a test in English today. What am I gonna tell Mrs. Hoople if you don't show?"

"Tell her the big, dumb Huckaby isn't coming."

Matt blows the air from his lungs. "Look, I don't mind that you're number one."

"*Right.*"

"No, really," he says. "I've been thinking about it—a lot. So come on, get out of bed."

"Go away, Matt." He doesn't move.

"Um, what about your stuff—your running-away stuff? If Dad finds it, he's gonna know. That would hurt him bad—Mom too. How about I put it in the shed, mix it in with the other things. You can do what you want with it later."

"Whatever," I say.

"Okay then."

Thumps come from the storage boxes as he drags

my escape gear out. From under my quilt, I see him put my money stash in my desk drawer.

"Oh, and Mom sent up some apple juice. I set it on your table. I'll, uh, I'll tell Mrs. Hoople you'll make up the test tomorrow."

"Go. Away."

11:38 A.M.

"I brought you some soup and a sandwich," Lizzie says. "And your favorite cookies. Chocolate chip."

"Not hungry."

"You have to eat, Frankie Joe. All you've had is a little apple juice—"

"I said I'm not hungry."

"I have to go to work now," she sighs. "But I'll leave the lunch on your table. Maybe you'll feel like eating later."

Wednesday, March 17

5:30 P.M.

"Hey, Oddball. Thought you was never gonna wake up." Mandy's sitting cross-legged on the foot of my bed. Her hair is done up in two ponytails, one over each ear. She looks like a pug-nosed Pekinese dog.

"Go away, Mandy."

"Can't. I'm here on official business. Your dad sent up a fresh bottle of water with orders for you to drink it." She points to the bottle on my nightstand.

"And Mrs. Bixby ordered you to come back to The Great Escape because she needs her assistant." She shakes her head. "Things are nuts again."

She pulls a piece of paper from her pocket. "And Miss Peachcott gave me this to read to you because she's crippled up and can't climb the stairs."

"Don't care."

"Too bad so sad, you're gonna hear it anyway." She unfolds the paper and begins to read: " 'Our customers need their deliveries and I need my tester.' " She pauses. "What the heck's a tester?"

"Go away, Mandy." I pull the covers over my head.

"But what am I supposed to tell Mrs. Bixby and Miss Peachcott? They're expecting me to tell them something."

"Don't care." The bed squeaks as she climbs off of it, but I don't hear the stairs creak. She hasn't left yet.

"Hey look," she mumbles, "I'm real sorry I called you that name when you wouldn't run against Matt. I didn't know that you had problems—more problems."

Swell. Now it's all over town that my mom dumped me just like her aunt Gerry dumped her.

"Go away!"

"Okay, okay!"

I wait for the stairs to creak. They don't. From under the corner of my quilt, I see Mandy standing at the top of the stairs.

"I really really miss you, Frankie Joe," she whispers.

I pull the quilt over my head again. Finally the stairs creak.

Friday, March 19

8: 17 A.M.

I'm skinny again. FJ and Lizzie asked Dr. Davis to make a house call today. I've been poked and prodded and thumped.

"He's worked awful hard," Lizzie tells the doctor. "And been out in the weather."

"And studying a lot," FJ says. "I pushed him too hard."

Dr. Davis closes his doctor bag and motions them toward the stairs.

"He's suffering from sadness," I hear him tell FJ and Lizzie as they clomp their way downstairs. "You need to do something to pull him out of the dumps. Not all wounds show up on the outside."

10:15 A.M.

"I drove twenty-five miles to get these," FJ says. "Stored them on ice. I, uh, I remembered you liked them when we drove up from Texas. One's an Oreo cookie and the other's an M&M."

He sets two Blizzards on the bedside table and leaves. They melt into goo.

12:15 P.M.

Matt, Mark, Luke, and Little Johnny bring me a chocolate-covered pretzel from the gift shop.

"Not hungry," I tell them, and pull the covers over my head.

As soon as they're gone, I toss the pretzel into the wastebasket.

2:20 P.M.

"Miss Peachcott sent these," Lizzie says. She shows me apples and plums and tangerines. "She said you liked colorful things."

"I think I'm gonna throw up," I tell her.

She takes the fruit away.

4:27 P.M.

"Mr. Puffin sent up a pizza," FJ says. "Your favorite—pepperoni with extra cheese."

"Can't," I mumble.

"Look," he says. "I know you're disappointed—and hurt. You have every right to be, but that's part of life. You have to learn to deal with it. That's what being an adult is all about. Remember our talk about responsibility?"

I pull a pillow over my head.

"Maybe later," he says, sighing. He sets the pizza on the steam radiator to keep it warm. It curls up into a Frisbee.

Saturday, March 20

3:30 P.M.

"Wake up, Frankie Joe." FJ gives me a shake.

"Not...hungry." I'm not lying. My lips are cracked, and my stomach feels hollow, but I can't stand the thought of eating.

"I didn't bring food. The postmaster is here with me. She called to tell me a package came for you today and she worked late so she could deliver it."

"It came all the way from Texas," the postmaster says.

Mom sent me a package! I feel an emptiness in my chest when I remember that Mom isn't in Texas anymore.

"It's from the Lone Star Trailer Park," FJ says, "and it's been sent Registered Mail—Restricted Delivery."

"That means you have to sign for it—personally," the postmaster says.

"That's right." FJ slides my pillows behind my back so I have to sit up. "It's time to buck up. Now sign for this package."

The postmaster hands me a ballpoint pen and yellow receipt, and points to where I'm supposed to sign.

"Okay," she says, after I sign my name, "the package is officially delivered." Turning to FJ, she says, "I'll show myself out."

"Must be important to send it Registered Mail." FJ hands me the package. "Cost a pretty penny to do that."

Looking at the stamps on the package, I calculate the postage. Holy cow! Twelve dollars and forty-nine cents!

The package is the size and shape of a shoe box. The outside is wrapped in a brown paper bag that has been cut apart and smoothed out and taped up with silver duct tape. The return address says, "Lone Star Trailer Park, Laredo, Texas."

FJ helps me peel off the duct tape and brown paper and, indeed, there is a shoe box inside. And inside the box is a rock.

I examine the rock. It's not granite, or quartz, or sandstone—

I catch my breath. No, he didn't . . . it can't be—

"Ohmigosh," I blurt out, "it's a space rock. He found it!"

"Space rock?"

"Yeah. It's part of a meteor."

"There's a note, too," FJ says. "From a Mrs. Jones, a Mr. O'Hare, and a Mr. Lopez?"

"They're my friends."

"If it's okay with you, I'd like to hear what they have to say."

He hands me the note, and I read it aloud.

Dearest Frankie Joe,

We are so sorry we didn't write sooner, but we kept hearing rumors that your mother was getting out of jail early, so we thought you would be back home soon. We looked for you every day. But when your mother pulled up stakes, she told us you wouldn't be returning at all. We didn't know what to think because we had all gotten Christmas cards that said you would be coming to see us soon. We decided not to wait any longer to give this to you, and we hope you keep your promise to come see us. We will look forward to that day.

Your friends,
Mrs. Jones, Mr. O'Hare, and Mr. Lopez.

"You promised your friends that you'd come see them?"

"Yes sir . . . sort of."

"I see." He takes the rock from my hand and examines it. "So this is really from outer space?"

"A meteor broke apart over the Chihuahua Desert last year. Mr. O'Hare and me have been looking for pieces of it for a long time."

"Amazing!" he says, handing the rock back to me.

4:10 P.M.

After FJ leaves, I carry my space rock to my desk. I feel shaky all over, like a bobble-head doll on the dashboard of a car. A spot between my eyes throbs like a tom-tom.

Opening the curtains, I realize that the days have gotten much longer. In the late afternoon light, the rock actually looks alien. It's not exactly brown, or black, or yellow. And it's heavy for something that's the size of a hockey puck.

"Wow," I say, talking to the space rock like it's Mr. O'Hare. "Wish I coulda been there when you found it." I look through the window again, feeling sad.

The outside world is turning green again. But all I can see is the bitter winter I've spent here in Clearview. The freezing cold, the deep snow, the ice crystals, the smothering gray. My skin turning tough as boot leather...my lungs aching as if they would burst...my leg muscles cramping from all the pumping. I see and feel and taste all of it again. And I know that none of it was what made me sick.

I begin to cry. I cry a flood, but the tears are not for my wasted planning and hard work. Or for all the anger I've had against FJ and my mutant ninja posse and their cruel nicknames.

I cry because Mom sold her remembrance of me.

Monday, April 5

4:15 P.M.

"Thanks, Frankie Joe," Mr. Puffin says. "Sure glad you're delivering pizza again."

"Me too." I look at the thermometer as I walk down his porch steps. Fifty-three degrees.

It's the first day of spring break, so I'm in no hurry to head back to Clearview. Mr. Puffin and Mr. Lindholm were my only deliveries today. They're working hard planting corn and soybeans.

The bike trip out was pretty tiring, but I'm almost good as new. After I got all that sadness out of me, I started eating again—and no one stays skinny in Lizzie's house for very long. I've started delivering for Miss Peachcott, too. I'm saving my money for our vacation. Dad and I are taking Lizzie and my brothers to see the Lone Star State of Texas. And I'm keeping the promise I made to go see my friends. Dad's real big on a person keeping his promises.

I hear yelling come from behind me. Pulling off, I wait for Matt to catch up.

"Hey," he says, pulling up next to me. He looks at the pizza container strapped to my bike basket. "You done with your deliveries?"

"Yep."

"Where you going now?"

"Nowhere special."

"Mind if I tag along."

"Nope." I start pedaling again.

"Let's go this way," Matt says after we've ridden a couple of miles. He swerves onto the two-lane highway that leads into Clearview.

I swerve onto the highway, too, and catch up with him. We have to ride on the shoulder to avoid traffic. Matt in front; me behind.

I call out, "Why are you going this way? The shoulder's gotta be rough on those skinny tires." Matt glances over his shoulder, grinning like a monkey.

What's he up to? . . .

When we reach the green-and-white sign that reads Clearview, he suddenly stops in front of me, forcing both of us into the ditch.

"Are you crazy? I almost crashed into that sign!"

"I figured you'd be sure to see it that way," Matt says. The monkey-face grin shows up again.

I look at the sign that reads BUSINESSES IN CLEARVIEW. A new business has been added to the list in fresh red paint: FRANKIE JOE'S FREAKY FAST DELIVERY SERVICE.

"Huh," I grunt, feeling a grin spread across my face.

"Race you home," Matt says, peeling off down the highway.

"No fair!" I yell. "You got a head start."

I see Huckaby Number Two pumping for all he's worth, so I take off, too. I smell the rain that's fallen on the newly planted corn and soybeans, and feel my leg muscles rippling beneath my jeans. I fly past the arrow-straight rows and pencil-line roads, sunshine warming the top of my head and shoulders. If I had wings, I just know I could fly.

In my mind's eye, I lift off the ground and rise above a patchwork of squares the color of soybean green and corn gold and Harvestore blue and barn red. I see myself flying over Wisconsin, which is only five miles to the north, where everything is a buttery yellow. Next I'm over Alberta and the Canadian Rockies, which are colored an icy blue. When I reach the edge of the Arctic, I see the purest white I've ever seen—even whiter than Miss Peachcott's hair. And then I reach the Arctic Circle and...

At the Arctic Circle, I see myself transported into a rocket ship that is fueled with corn and heading to places that aren't on any maps. There isn't even a color for that place "out there."

But I'm not afraid because I know I won't get lost. All I have to do is follow the road map of colors... back home.